LOST

BETH YARNALL

LOST

---

ebook ISBN: 9781940811994

print ISBN: 9781940811567

To my husband, Mr Y, for buying into and supporting every single one of my crazy Lucy and Ethel schemes...including the one where I thought I could write a book.

Miyuki Price-Jones held up the shocking pink Multiple O vibrator, flipped the switch and... nothing. No reversible rotating head, no quivering bunny ears and no massaging beads. For the third time this week she'd turned on a toy only to end up frustrated.

"Davy!" Crosby yelled from somewhere in the darkened television studio.

The young man in the corner jumped, then shuffled over to the man sitting in a faded director's chair. "Yes, Mr. Crosby?"

"Your job is simple. Put the batteries in the toys, test them to make sure they work and don't give me a reason to kick your ass all the way to Tuscaloosa!" Rob Crosby, the director of the adult home shopping show, *Pleasure at Home*, pinched the bridge of his nose.

All Miyuki, or Mi, could see was the top of Crosby's balding head, but she could tell he'd had it with Davy. He was going to fire him even though none of this was his fault. It was sabotage... again. She set the Multiple O vibrator down on the faux walnut coffee table next to the other sex toys she would be showcasing today and stood to get Crosby's attention. "I'm sure it's not Davy's fault. Maybe we got a bad batch of batteries. Or—"

"Or more likely Davy is an incompetent idiot who couldn't find his own ass with both hands and a map!" Crosby shouted. Crosby was always shouting. It had taken Mi three weeks to stop flinching every time he opened his mouth. Crosby turned on Davy. "Did you even *put* batteries in it?"

Davy bobbed his head. "Yes, sir."

Without wavering his glare at Davy, Crosby barked, "Check it, Mi. And so help me Davy." Crosby pointed a finger at the young man. "If four double A's don't pop out the bottom of that thing your ass is grass." Someone's ass was always grass or otherwise in jeopardy with Crosby.

Mi picked up the Multiple O and opened the bottom of it. Four batteries sat there, nestled properly with the plus and minus ends exactly as they should be. "Davy's right. There must be something wrong with the batteries." She tipped the device upright and switched it on. Still nothing. "Or the vibrator."

Crosby threw the sheaf of papers in his hands, sending them floating down around him. "God damn it! Somebody get me some goddamned batteries that work! Of all the incompetent, backwoods, inbred—"

"Crosby?" Mi interrupted. "Why don't I just take the batteries from one of the other—"

"Davy can do it!" Crosby stood up. "Take five, everybody. When I get back every single one of those goddamned things better work. Or your ass is hitting the pavement. Hear me, Davy? And somebody pick up those goddamned papers." He turned and stormed off in the direction of the studio offices. "Mi! With me."

Mi handed the Multiple O to Davy with a mumbled apology. Even though there was often no good excuse for Crosby's bad behavior, she still felt like she had to apologize for him.

Davy waved it off as most did when she made the gesture, his long blond hair hanging like a curtain as he bent over his task. "Ain't your fault, Miss Mi. Better catch up before he starts threatenin' you, too."

Mi turned to follow Crosby and caught sight of a man she'd never seen before, standing against the wall just out of the reach of the stage lights, his face fully shadowed. He was large, well over six feet tall and as broad as a doublewide. Something about the way he stoodstill, yet humming with energy caused an answering rhythm to thrum from deep inside her. Her pulse kicked up, generating a near fight or flight sensation that sent her senses into overdrive. Who was he? What was he doing here?

"Mi!"

She jumped, her focus flickering to Crosby, then back to the man. "Coming," she answered, keeping her gaze on the man.

She rounded the end of the stage opposite him and stepped down. The man made no move, but she knew he watched her. Turning down the hall after Crosby, she should have felt relieved to be out of the man's sight and yet she instantly missed the extra beat his attention had caused.

Crosby sat at his desk, pulling a long drink from the flask he kept in his bottom drawer. He wiped away the bright pink drop from his bottom lip, but not before Mi had seen it. He thought he was fooling everyone by putting stomach medicine in a container meant for alcohol. And he was. Everyone, but Mi.

He looked up at her with blurry, red eyes. "Third time this week." He held up a hand. "Before you say it, I know. It's not Davy. But goddamn it, I hate this shit." He leaned back in his chair and waved for Mi to sit down, so she did. "The police don't have one single lead and I know you're not going to like it, but Sellers hired you a bodyguard."

She opened her mouth to protest, but was cut off.

"Goddamn it, don't fight me on this. It's a done deal. With Lucy out on maternity leave, you're all we've got. And there's no way Sellers is going to stop shooting the show for one single goddamned day. You got me? You're cash in the bank. Ratings haven't budged an inch since Lucy got too big to hock dildos, proving you're the real draw, not her." He waved an idle hand around. "Must be that ancient Chinese secret thing or something. Hell, I don't know. All I know is that Sellers protects his investments and right now, you're investment number one."

Mi would have corrected him that she was one-quarter Japanese and not at all Chinese, but she knew he didn't care. That wasn't the point. A bodyguard. She didn't like the sound of that. A bodyguard meant real danger and she didn't think a handful of threatening letters and one or two random acts of vandalism warranted a rent-a-cop.

"But Detective Rolls said it was probably a couple of over zealous members of that religious group, C.A.L.M. Unless something's changed that I don't know about." She searched Crosby's face and instantly knew she hadn't been fully informed. "What aren't you telling me?"

"Shit." Crosby dropped his gaze to a paper on his desk, pausing for a moment like he was making an important decision. "I don't want to scare you, kid, but I suppose you'd find out about it sooner or later." He lifted the top couple of papers, then carefully slid out an envelope and handed it to her. "These are copies of what was handed over to the police."

Mi didn't comment on how much his hand shook when she took the envelope from him. That small tremor sent her nerves jangling. If Crosby was this upset over what was inside the envelope, then it had to be bad. Very bad.

She braced for it, but the reality of what she had to face was worse than she ever could have imagined. She flipped through the photos, one after the other, caught by the snippets of her life that had been well documented on film. Her unlocking her car in front of her house, in the produce section of the grocery store, in line at the dry cleaners, sitting in a church pew, holding a box of tampons in the drug store, having lunch with Lucy. And the final one—the one that had her clutching at her chest—was of her and her mother, feeding the ducks in the park under a hot Texas sun with the baby stroller parked close by.

She looked up to find Crosby watching her closely. "Are you okay, kid?"

She shook her head, unable to form the words she had for the emotions welling up inside her, trying to claw their way out.

"In that case, let me introduce Lucas Vega. Your bodyguard."

She jerked in surprise, turning her head to the side, then up, way up. That low hum started again at the sight of the still man from the studio. He stood feet above her, looking down at her with no emotion. Certainly, nothing like the sensations clanging around inside her caused by his nearness. He was dark, like a shadow, dressed in all black with black hair and near black eyes. And not at all handsome. Which strangely made him more attractive to her.

Mi clutched the photos tighter. "No."

"Sellers owns this station and all our asses. There is no 'no'." And then Crosby said something he avoided as though it gave him a violent rash. "Sorry, kid."

She knew there was no way out. Those two simple words sounded with a thud in her head, like a trunk lid closing with her inside.

"She's a peach once you get to know her," Crosby said to Lucas, standing. "I'll leave you two to get acquainted and to make sure Davy's finally unscrewed his screw up." Crosby pointed at Mi. "Three minutes and then I want you back on set twirling dildos. Jesus, if my mother could see me," Crosby mumbled to the ceiling as he left the room.

Lucas wasn't sure what to say. Miyuki Price-Jones off camera was nothing like he'd thought she'd be. First off, she was small, too small, looking more like a teenager than the twenty-eight her file said she was. He knew she wore the glasses for the sex-kitten effect on the show, but what the file hadn't said was what a strange color her eyes were, gold, like an old coin.

The file also hadn't said anything about her having a kid. He wondered why. It wasn't like her reputation would be compromised. She sold sex toys for fuck's sake. Something told him that her having a kid would add a complication he wasn't sure he wanted to deal with. Must have been why Cal Sellers had left that bit of information out of the file. And why Lucas would look into it as soon as he got the chance.

She didn't speak or pay him any attention at all as she shoved the photos back into the envelope, her movements jerky and rushed. Then she sat there, holding the envelope, staring at it as though she didn't know what to do with it.

"May I?"

She jolted at his question, spinning in her chair. She eyed his outstretched hand as if he'd strike her with it. That thought made him frown.

She clasped the photos to her chest. "No."

He withdrew his hand, disguising his uneasiness at her reaction to him with a careless shrug. He was used to people making judgments about him. Usually he spun those misconceptions to his advantage, but for some reason her negative assessment of him rankled. He told himself it was better this way. Her discomfort meant she'd take direction from him if things got bad. And that was good.

"I'm sorry, Mr. Vega." She rose to face him.

The first thing he noticed was that she was a little taller than she first appeared. The next thing he noticed was that despite her paleness from shock, her spine was straight, her chin high. It would take a lot to really rattle Ms. Price-Jones. That, too, was good. Maybe this favor he was doing for Cal wouldn't be so bad.

"I didn't mean to be rude." She indicated the pictures. "It's just that these are personal."

"It would help me to know what we're dealing with." The truth was he wanted to study them more closely than the glimpse he'd gotten over her shoulder. He told himself they would tell him more about who might be after Ms. Price-Jones, but the real truth was he wanted to know more about *her*.

She frowned down at the envelope. "Oh."

"And please, call me Lucas."

"Lucas." She said it as if she were trying it out to see how the letters felt on her tongue. Which brought his attention to her mouth and its fullness. Her tongue darted out, leaving her lower lip wet.

He had the strongest urge to run his thumb across it just to see how it felt.

"How does this work? This bodyguard thing?"

Lucas brought his attention back to her eyes, which were wide behind her fake glasses. With fear or something else? He couldn't be sure. He wanted to put her at ease. He almost reached out to touch her, but wasn't entirely sure she wouldn't bolt if he did. Instead he shifted his stance, trying for reassuring.

"I'm with you twenty-four, seven. I go where you go."

"Oh." She didn't look reassured. If anything she looked more agitated.

"You won't even know I'm there."

She gave a shaky laugh. "I seriously doubt that. You're awfully hard to miss."

"What I mean is you'll go about your day same as always."

"Except for my very large shadow."

He cracked a hint of a smile. "Yes."

She smiled in return and then the most remarkable thing happened. She touched him, taking his hand in hers. "Well, then, nice to meet you, Lucas. Please, call me Mi."

"Mi." It was his turn to try out her name, and he liked the way it made him feel.

She released his hand. He missed the contact.

"I'd better get back before Crosby starts yelling." She looked at the envelope again, a frown creasing her brow. And then she thrust it at him, hitting him mid chest. "Here." She released it without waiting for him to bring his hand up. He grabbed it before it hit the ground. "When you're done, burn them. Shred them. I don't care." But she didn't look at them as though she didn't care. "I don't want to see them again."

That he believed, and he wanted to be the one to make them go away for her. He wasn't sure why he felt a protectiveness toward her that went beyond his job description. A protectiveness that was entirely personal. He wanted to be the shield that separated her from the things that made her eyes wide with fear and had her flinching at an outstretched hand.

Lucas tucked the envelope into the inside pocket of his leather jacket and followed Mi back to the studio where it looked as though they had gotten everything straightened out. People milled about, checking or testing things, shouting out and answering commands. He felt out of place here. Everything was so fake: the seating group meant to look like anyone's living room, the backdrop with a windowed view of anyone's neighborhood and the woman standing in the midst of it all, getting her hair and makeup touched up. Mi.

Gone was the reserved, almost shy, woman he'd met earlier. In her place was the on-camera siren who sold sex toys, handling them like a pro. That thought made his shoulders twitch. Would he be the first to assume a woman who sold sex toys also had vast intimate knowledge of how to use them? What kind of crazy kink would a woman like her be into? Watching her switch on a vibrator and stroke the shaft while extolling its virtues affected him more than he wanted it to. More than it should have. He wondered if he was the only one getting turned on by her display. He'd bet not. A woman like her would have men tripping themselves to get to her.

But there had been no reference of a husband, boyfriend or any other kind of personal relationship in her file. Maybe there were too many to mention. He shifted his feet, more uncomfortable with that notion than he had a right to be. He thought again of the photo of Mi and another woman by a lake with a baby stroller. The other woman looked too old to be the mother of an infant. So if the baby wasn't Mi's, whose was it? And where was the baby's father?

Mi held up two odd looking things with small clamps. "Next up we have a beautiful set of cordless vibrating nipple clamps from Love's Slave. Foreplay fun or masturbation enhancement, these lovely vibrating clamps are made of soft, supple rubber and are adjustable for your pleasure. Tickle, tease and please your perky tips hands-free, batteries included..."

Jesus. Lucas's gaze immediately dropped to Mi's breasts as she spoke. He first imagined using the nipple clamps on her, but quickly discarded that image, replacing it with his hands and mouth, licking and coaxing her nipples to stiff peaks...

"Increase your orgasmic pleasure by combining your Love's Slave vibrating nipple clamps with the vibrator or dildo of your choice. Only twenty-nine, ninety-nine and available in three colors: pink, purple and silver..."

He'd like to increase *her* orgasmic pleasure and not with some battery operated contraption, but with hands and tongue and the slide of skin on skin. He pictured his hands pressed to her small breasts, his thumbs tracing circles around her aroused flesh...

"Also from Love's Slave we have the Ride 'Em Cowgirl, a stationary ride-on vibe with three speeds. Just place the Ride 'Em Cowgirl on your bed or floor and set your own pace, slow and sensual or fast and hard. However you like it, you decide…"

A fine sweat coated Lucas's forehead and upper lip. He adjusted the front of his pants, picturing Mi naked, rising over him, riding *him* like a cowgirl…

"This bubble gum pink ride-on vibe has adjustable speeds and a strong suction cup attachable to any surface for when you want to ride doggie-style…"

Fuck. His hands flexed at his sides as he pictured Mi on all fours in front of him. He gripped her hips, taking her hard and fast from behind just the way he'd like…

"Don't forget tonight's show special: Decadence's Heart-on For You, a beautiful hand-blown glass phallus with a heart shaped handle and sensual beads for added stimulation. And *Pleasure at Home's* own Slippery When Whet, a water-based, non-stain lubricant to enhance your sexual experience. Regularly fifty-nine…"

Was she wet right now? Did she get turned on, handling the long hard shafts, describing how to use them? Did she pleasure herself in the darkness of her bedroom late at night?

"We also have some wonderful products for gentlemen, beginning with the Super Stroker 3000 from Midnight Embrace." Mi held up some kind of tube-looking device. "Extra long to accommodate any sized man, this deep throated stroker will bring you to completion and beyond. Soft, full lips wrap around your shaft, gently sucking…"

He'd experienced less painful torture in the Navy. Watching Mi's sales pitch was the most erotic thing he'd seen in a long time. And it had been way too long since he'd had anything, but his own hand to slake his lust. He shifted his feet and looked around, needing another focus for his attention. He wanted to fill a sink and dunk his head, give it a good solid soak for the things he'd been thinking. Instead he let his gaze wander the studio, studying the layout, the exits, and the people. He catalogued everything, storing the knowledge away. He was here to protect Mi, nothing more. If only he could erase the erotic images that flickered across his mind like a porno movie.

Damn Cal and his stupid favor.

AN HOUR LATER, Mi wrapped up the show by repeating *Pleasure at Home's* two phone numbers—one for women and one for men—and reminded her viewers that they could view all of tonight's products and more online on *Pleasure at Home's* website.

"That's a wrap," Crosby shouted.

Mi stepped off the stage, glad to be out of the glare of the lights that seemed sharper with the headache hovering at the back of her head. Her gaze automatically wandered the far corners of the studio, looking for Lucas. She found him near the door, arms folded over his chest. She could just make out his dark shape in the shadows. He looked more imposing than ever. She remembered how gentle, almost kind, he'd been with her earlier. The contrast in him gave her shivers.

She handed Tracey, the makeup artist, her on-show, trademark eyeglasses. It had been Mr. Sellers's idea for her to wear them even though she had perfect eyesight. He'd thought the sexy librarian look would be a perfect contrast to Lucy's blond bombshell. She missed Lucy. Doing the show without her wasn't as much fun, but with just weeks left of her pregnancy, Lucy didn't fit *Pleasure at Home's* provocative image. A hugely pregnant woman wasn't sexy, according to Mr. Sellers.

Mi and Tracey headed to the makeup room just off the main studio. *Pleasure at Home* was wildly successful, but not successful enough for anything more than a glorified closet as a makeup room. Tracey pulled the bobby pins from Mi's hair while Mi attacked her face with a baby wipe. She hated the thick pancake makeup required for on-camera work. Tracey finished brushing out Mi's hair just as Mi wiped the last of the makeup and cold cream off with a tissue.

Tracey set down the hairbrush and began cleaning up the makeup counter. "You're all set, Mi."

"Thanks, Tracey," Mi said as she gathered her things. "I'll see you tomorrow." She turned to find Lucas crowding the doorway. "Oh! Hello." Had he been there the whole time?

He examined her face as though it was a riddle that needed solving. "You have freckles," he whispered more to himself than her.

Mi lowered her head a little, touching a finger to her lightly speckled nose. She hated her freckles. "Yeah, since I was a kid," she answered just as quietly.

"Hmm."

She couldn't tell if that was a good 'hmm' or a bad 'hmm'. He continued to study her face, his gaze tracing over every inch as though it intrigued him. She knew she looked much different without the makeup, which exaggerated the almond shape of her eyes, the fullness of her lips and the sharpness of her cheekbones. Most men only saw the sex kitten who sold personal pleasure devices, expecting her to be wild in bed. Her on-camera self was sexy and sought after, but her off-camera self was freckled and easily skipped over.

She didn't know why the way he looked at her now made her feel apologetic, it just did. And it annoyed her. "It's the makeup. I'm supposed to look the part." She dropped her voice further until it was barely audible. "You know, seductive and alluring."

He frowned, a deep V forming between his brows.

"Mi, you forgot this." Tracey held out Mi's cell phone, angling herself for an introduction to Lucas.

"Thank you. Tracey Casey meet Lucas Vega my—" And then it slipped out, catching Mi as unaware as anyone. "—boyfriend," she finished, not daring to look at Lucas. What had she just done?

"Pleased to meet you," Lucas said smoothly, as though it were true.

"Boyfriend?" She could feel Tracey's questioning stare, but she didn't dare look up.

"Yes, ah—"

Lucas cut in. "We've just made it official."

And then Lucas draped his arm across her shoulders, bringing her up against his side. A decidedly hot and altogether hard side. She could smell the leather of his coat mixed with the fundamental scent of warm male. It was all she could do to not turn her head and rub her face against his chest, luxuriating in his scent like a bitch in heat. Instead she brought her arm up and under his jacket, laying her hand flat on his lower back just above the hard ridge of what was probably a gun. More heat. His muscles twitched under her palm.

Tracey tipped her head back and to one side. "Well then, congratulations. I suppose."

Mi was surprised at the tone Tracey used. If she didn't know better, she would have thought Tracey was being catty.

"Thank you. Well, we'd better go. See you tomorrow," Mi told her.

Lucas navigated them through the doorway. Mi bunched a handful of his t-shirt in her fist to keep up with him. Once they were clear of Tracey, Lucas leaned down and whispered in her ear, his lips brushing her hair. "Nice explanation."

"I didn't know what to say. How to explain."

"I'm not complaining. It's the perfect excuse for us to be together twenty-four seven."

She could have sworn he smoothed his cheek away more slowly than necessary. And he might have taken an extra deep breath while he did so.

"So you're okay with that?" She hoped he was because they were getting looks on their way back through the studio, walking with their arms around each other.

"Sure. Unless you already have a boyfriend."

Her answer came out rushed. "No. No boyfriend."

"What the hell?" Crosby said from behind them.

They'd almost made it to the door when Crosby called them back. "Mi, in my office. Now!"

Mi would have dropped her arm, turning to go back was the perfect excuse, but Lucas still held her to him.

"Get in here and close the door." Crosby waited while they crowded into his office, which wasn't much bigger than the makeup room. Crosby gestured back and forth between them. "What the hell is all this?"

Lucas dropped his arm, forcing Mi to do the same. "Appearances. Unless you want everyone to know Mi has a bodyguard?"

"No. I suppose not." Crosby never looked happy, but this was a new level of displeasure even for Crosby. "You're gonna watch where you put your hands. You get me?"

Lucas tucked his hands in his pockets. "Yes, sir."

"Crosby." Mi's cheeks heated. She felt about sixteen, going on her first date.

"There are a bunch of goddamned protesters out front, more than usual," Crosby said. "Sellers hired a couple of guards for outside, but I wanted to give you the heads up. The lady from C.A.L.M. is out there with a goddamned megaphone, stirring up all kinds of shit."

"C.A.L.M.?" Lucas asked.

"Christians Against Loose Morals," Mi explained. She tried not to show how much it bothered her that Cookie Dixon and her group picketed every show taping or that their numbers seemed to be growing every week. When she met Crosby's eyes and saw the softening of his expression, she knew she hadn't pulled it off.

"It'll be all right, kid. You're well protected." Crosby sent Lucas a look, communicating something Mi didn't catch. "Investment number one, remember? Here's your mail." He handed a stack of envelopes to Lucas. "I know you like to answer your fan mail, but from here on out, he goes through it with you. Anything that's off gets bagged and goes to Detective Rolls. Got it?" Crosby said more to Lucas than Mi. "Now get out of here."

They did as Crosby said, exiting the building through a side entrance near where Mi had parked her car. The building that housed the *Pleasure at Home* studio and offices looked like every other building in the huge industrial complex just outside of Dallas.

The air hung heavy with the heat of the dying day. The last rays of the sun slashed the sky orange and red, foretelling another day of oppressive summer tomorrow. They could hear the crowd on the other side of the building, sending up cheers after everything Cookie Dixon said through her megaphone. Mi tried not to let the negativity and hatred get to her, but it was hard when so much of it was often directed at her as one of the faces of *Pleasure at Home*.

Lucas held out his hand. "Give me your keys."

"Why?"

They'd reached Mi's car, a compact sedan that looked like every other vehicle in the parking lot, and faced off on the driver's side of the car.

"I drive," Lucas insisted.

"This is my car."

"For me to do my job I'm going to need you to do

what I say. Sometimes I'll be able to give you a reason, sometimes not."

"So what's your reason?"

He looked at her for a moment like he wouldn't answer, challenging her to go along without having to give her a reason. Then he seemed to come to some kind of decision. "I'd feel weird having you drive me around."

She dropped the keys into his palm. "That's as good a reason as any, I suppose."

He walked her around to her side of the car and opened the door for her. She saw him flick a look at the car seat in the back and cringed inside, anticipating his questions. Instead he closed the door without comment, which felt almost like he'd closed off a part of himself.

He climbed into the driver's seat with difficulty, his knees up near his chin. Mi smothered a laugh. He finally got the seat adjusted as far back as it would go, but his legs were still too long.

"Damn compacts," he muttered.

This time Mi didn't bother hiding her chuckle. "I can drive."

"We'll be taking my truck going forward."

He pulled out of the parking space. They drove around the building and got their first look at the mass of people gathered outside the gates of the parking lot. Cookie stood on something to make her taller than the crowd that jabbed picket signs in the air, shouting in response to the things she said. There were more than ever before and their signs were more sophisticated.

This was a new kind of crowd—organized and more dangerous than the Sunday school teachers and PTA parents who usually protested.

Suddenly a loud crack rent the air. The back window exploded behind them, pelting them with glass.

"Get down," Lucas ordered, shoving Mi's head between her knees. He hit the gas pedal, sending them straight at the crowd blocking their exit.

2

Mi's face paled, making her freckles stand out in stark relief. If it was possible, she looked even smaller, more fragile. Lucas wanted to reach out to her, take her hand in his, and pull her to him.

"I need to see the other letters. Where are they?" Lucas asked as gently as he knew how.

She swayed where she stood and that's when Lucas did what he'd wanted to do since he met her. He stood, sweeping her off her feet and into his arms, then settled back onto the chair in one fluid motion. Shivering, she snuggled into him as though she needed his heat to ward off the cold. He held her as tightly as he dared, acutely aware of the difference in their sizes. She slid her arms around his neck and pressed closer. She seemed to need something from him, something he wasn't giving.

"Tighter," she whispered, grabbing handfuls of his t-shirt.

He repositioned his arms, doing his best to do what she asked and at the same time trying not to crush her. She was softer than he thought she'd be, the feel her skin, the lushness of her flesh. He lowered his chin, resting it against her hair still damp from her shower. She smelled like a flower garden, clean and feminine to the extreme. He ached to press his nose to her neck, between her breasts. Hell, he wanted to taste her. Just once.

He shifted her slightly, relieving the pressure of her hip against his erection. One of her hands slipped down his chest. She flattened her palm, moving it over him slowly, experimentally. Her breath blew hot against his neck. He wondered what she thought of him, of his size. He held still, hardly breathing, afraid she'd stop touching him. More than anything he wanted her hands on him. All over him.

The fingers of her other hand laced into the hair at the nape of his neck, tentatively at first and then she grew bolder, stroking him. He suppressed a moan, chills racing over his body. It took every ounce of his military training to remain perfectly motionless. This tiny woman had reduced him to a quivering mass of need with nothing more than her touch. And then she brushed her lips on his neck in a barely there kiss that was nearly his undoing.

"I'm sorry," she whispered, pushing against his chest for him to release her.

It took a moment for his arms to obey. He loosened his grip and she slipped right out, moving out of his arms and away from him as fast as she could. He felt the loss as though she'd been ripped from him.

She wouldn't look at him past his chin. "Thank you. You know—" She gestured at him. "—for that. I'll just go and, ah, get you those letters." She disappeared down the hall.

He sat there, staring at the empty space where she'd stood, her scent still wrapped around him. One moment he was sitting, then the next he was following her. Down the hall to the one room he'd not been in. Hers. There was more of Mi here. Her fragrance. Her taste for soft colors and plush fabrics. He didn't see her at first and then noticed the light on in the closet. She mumbled to herself, moving things around. When he looked inside she was reaching up for a box on the top shelf.

He came up behind her and easily grabbed it for her. She gave a shriek of surprise and jumped back into him.

He wrapped an arm across her middle, bringing her against him and preventing her from falling. "Didn't mean to scare you." He presented her with the box, still holding her to him. "Is this what you were after."

She reached for it with both hands. "Yes. Thank you." She sounded a little breathless. A little nervous.

Was she afraid of him? That thought had him taking a step back, releasing her instantly. He backed away and into the bedroom.

She followed, the box tucked against her hip. She set the box on the bed and opened it. She riffled through it until she found what she was looking for, a small bundle of letters bound together. "These are all of them. I guess there were more than I thought."

There had to be at least ten letters in the bundle. Lucas accepted them with a frown. The oldest letter was postmarked a year ago. "You should have reported these. It might have made a difference at Doyle Gann's parole hearing."

She worked her lip between her teeth.

She looked so alone. Something about her had triggered all of his protective instincts from the moment he'd seen her at the TV studio. It wasn't her size or her situation, but something more fundamental. She was his responsibility. His to care for.

He tried for reassuring, anything to get her to stop gnawing her lip. "You don't worry about Doyle Gann or anything else. That's my job. You hear? You just go about your business, do your show. You'll be fine."

She gave a short nod and some of the strain in her face eased away.

Now that he'd touched her he couldn't seem to stop. Cupping her face in his hand he smoothed her worn lip. "That's better."

For the first time in maybe forever Mi felt like she wasn't alone. When Lucas had swept her up and cradled her in his arms, she'd felt cherished, protected. He'd done nothing more than comfort her even though he was obviously aroused. This man was a bundle of contradictions. Despite his size he was surprisingly gentle and moved with the grace and power of a predator. She knew he'd never harm her, but sensed he could be hurt very deeply. And now he was looking at her with a combination of protectiveness and a hunger so raw it reached inside her and scorched a path straight through her.

Nothing with this man would be simple or straightforward. It would be complicated, demanding and all consuming. But she didn't want easy. She wanted to be whisked away on a flood of desire so strong it stole her breath and blocked out all other thought.

She didn't know who moved first, but suddenly she was lifted up and into him. Wrapping her arms around his neck, she held him as fiercely as he held her. Their gazes locked. His eyes were dark with need, but he gave her that split second to back out, to change her mind. Then his mouth was on hers, moving with skill that only hinted at the passion he was capable of. She changed the angle of the kiss, wanting more. Thrusting her hands in his hair, she brought him closer.

They tumbled onto the bed and the playing field was even. She could move against him without the difference in their size interfering. Her hands roamed over the sharp angles of his face, down across his broad shoulders. He brought her up against him, lifting her leg over his hip. Pulling her head back by her hair, he broke the kiss, licking and nipping her neck. He was everywhere. She nearly forgot who she was and why this was probably not a good idea. She heard the faint peal of warning bells that sounded like her mother's ringtone.

She bolted upright. "Oh, my God. My phone."

Lucas leaned up on an elbow, his arm wrapped around her waist. "Let it ring."

"No." She scrambled out of bed, fumbling to right her robe. If she didn't answer it, her mother wouldn't just call back, she'd come over thinking something was wrong. Mi skidded to a stop in the kitchen and fumbled in her purse on the counter for her phone. The phone stopped ringing just as she found it.

"Damn it!" She punched in her mother's number, hopping foot to foot. "Come on, come on. Answer. Hello? Hi. No, sorry. I was in the bathroom."

Lucas came up behind her and put his arms around her, bending so he could lick the shell of her ear. "*Querida.*"

His murmur sent chills of pleasure racing through her. And then her mother said something that nearly stopped her heart.

"I think there's something wrong with Ethan."

Mi fumbled madly to get out of Lucas's embrace. She held a hand up to ward him off and backed away, trying to keep her voice even. "Why do you say that?" she asked her mother.

"He seems... I don't know—" Her mother's words slurred slightly. "—not right. The signs are all there like when I saw the rainbow in the window at Kroger's. Do you remember that?"

Lucas watched her with an intensity that unnerved her. She had to get away from him. He saw too much. More than she wanted him to.

"Hang on a minute," she told her mother. She put her hand over the phone and addressed Lucas in the calmest way she could without letting him see all of the stomach-turning turmoil inside of her. She indicated the phone. "I need to take this."

Fleeing back down the hall to her room, Mi prayed she could handle her mother with just a simple phone call. If not then she'd have to call her brother, Jason, and that was a conversation she did not want to have.

Lucas watched Mi escape back down the hall. Whoever was on the phone had said something that had scared her half to death. She'd looked at him like he was the enemy, panic clawing at her, draining her face of color. He'd give anything right that moment to find out whom she was speaking to and what they were saying. He reminded himself that he was just her bodyguard. His job was to keep her alive and nothing more. But with those few stolen kisses he *felt* like more.

Frustration burned a hole in his gut. This was supposed to have been an easy few days. Instead he had a dick hard enough to cut diamonds caused by a slip of a woman who drove him to near distraction. A woman who had secrets she wasn't likely to share with him. He sank into the nearest chair and looked around him. The house held few clues about the woman who owned it. If anything she became an ever-increasing mystery the more he knew about her.

He'd be wise to keep his distance from her. No more kisses, no more holding her, no more thoughts about the breast he'd gotten a peek of when her robe had slipped open. Small, almost dainty, and tipped with the most exquisitely sculpted pink nipple...

Fuck.

He got up and made the rounds of the house,

checking to make sure the locks were in place, pathetic as they were. This house was a security nightmare. Anybody with a boot could bust through the front door and to top it off the window over the kitchen sink wouldn't lock. He'd managed to jerry-rig it temporarily, but he didn't have much confidence in it. He could think of a hundred ways he could get in with nothing more than a screwdriver and his bare hands.

Confident the house was as secure as it could be, he stopped outside Mi's room to give her instructions so he could sneak in a quick shower. Her voice through the thin door stilled his hand before he could knock.

"No, you don't seem to get that this is your responsibility, too. I wasn't the only one there, you know... I'm doing the best I can, but I have to work to pay for things... I know, I know, but what am I supposed to do about that now?... Why can't you help me for once?... His birthday is next month. You are going to be there, aren't you?... Please, I can't do this alone."

There was a long pause in her conversation and then her wavering voice turned pleading, desperate.

"Please, Jay. Please. I need you."

He was an idiot to be getting involved with Mi. Standing outside her bedroom door listening while she begged another man, needing another man, he felt twelve times the fool. He knocked on her door anyway, banging on it hard out of spite. He heard a yelp of surprise that gave him a kind of perverse joy, then he heard her mumble something, probably to the asshole on the phone. She cracked the door open, peering wide-eyed at him like a child who'd been busted. He noticed she held the phone against her belly.

"I'm going to take a quick shower," he told her louder than was necessary, pushing past her into the room. "I need to check your window to make sure it's secure."

He made a show of checking her window, taking longer than he normally would. Which was probably why he noticed it. A small hole in the headrail of the aluminum mini blinds over the window. He inspected it as best as he could without disturbing it or giving away the fact that it had drawn his attention.

He backed away from the window and walked the room, casually looking for more holes or anything else that was unusual.

"What are you looking for?" Mi asked, biting her lip and clutching her phone tighter against her.

Noticing the hole in the smoke detector directly across from her bed, Lucas nearly cursed out loud. Someone had already broken into the house and set up cameras with a perfect view of everything Mi would have done in her bedroom, including changing her clothes and that brief roll on the bed with him. The thought of a stranger spying on Mi in her most private moments pissed him off so much it was all he could do not to hit something.

Mi must have caught on to his mood because she put the phone to her ear and told Jay the asshole she'd call him back. She dropped the phone into the pocket of her robe, and faced him fully, shoulders back, chin up.

"What's wrong?" she asked.

"I need you to get dressed and pack a bag with whatever you're going to need for a few days. Maybe a week."

"Why?"

Lucas debated telling her for two reasons. One: the fucker who'd been spying on her could be listening in. And two: he didn't want to scare her. She'd been though enough. More than enough.

But she also deserved to know what she was up against.

"Someone broke in to your house and installed cameras. There are two in here and if I looked, I imagine I'd find more." He'd bet money there'd be at least one, probably two in the bathroom. "The locks on your doors and windows are a joke. The lock on the window over the kitchen sink is broken. I can't adequately protect you here."

Trembling, she rubbed her forehead, working that bottom lip again. He wanted so much to go to her, put his arms around her and make it all go away.

"Where are they?" she asked, her voice sounding rusty and raw.

"At the window and the smoke detector." He clenched his jaw, thinking about how violated she must feel.

"How... how long do you think they've been there?"

"I don't know."

She nodded and walked to her dresser. She turned back, looking at him over her shoulder. "Where do I... how do I...?" Her voice cracked at first, then grew stronger as the anger came to her. "How am I supposed to dress knowing someone's watching me?"

"I'll check the closet, but I don't expect to find a camera there. You can take what you need and dress in there."

She turned back to the dresser and began pulling things out of drawers. Lucas went to the closet and searched everywhere he could think someone would hide a camera. He didn't find anything. He walked back into the bedroom and found Mi leaning over the dresser, her palms flat on the surface, supporting her weight. She'd stacked a few things on top, then seemed to have hit a wall. She breathed deeply in and out, her shoulders hunched. He could see just enough of her face in the mirror over the dresser to know she was fighting emotion. Since the moment he'd met her, he'd witnessed this slight warrior valiantly wage war on a whole barrage of feelings he couldn't begin to imagine.

He came up behind her and placed a hand on her shoulder. She turned into him instantly, wrapping her arms around his middle, holding on tight. He tucked her into him, helpless to stop himself. He didn't know what was or wasn't going on between them. All he knew was that she needed him. And in that moment it was enough.

He held her until she'd gotten her fill and pulled out of the embrace. She gathered her things and headed for the closet. His arms felt strangely empty without her in them so he crossed them over his chest. While he waited, he examined the items on her dresser. There were the usual female things: a hairbrush, some hair pins, a tube of lip stuff, a pair of earrings and framed photo of Mi and Lucy on the set of *Pleasure at Home*. It was a casual pose of the two of them with their arms around each other and smiles as wide and open as the Texas sky. Their friendship was obvious in the way their heads were tipped together.

His let his gaze wander the room, seeking out more information on Mi from the things she surrounded herself with. He told himself it was part of his training and would probably be with him the rest of his life. Focusing on the smallest pieces of the puzzle helped him visualize the whole. This he was good at. If only he had applied this skill to his personal life, then Cal wouldn't have had to be the one to tell him Vanessa was fucking around on him. In retrospect the signs had been there. He'd been an idiot to ignore them. He wouldn't be that idiot again.

Which brought him back to Mi. If this Jay was so important, where was he? Why wasn't he here taking care of her? And why if she needed Jay so much, did she turn to Lucas as if he was all she had in the world?

Forcing those thoughts aside for the time being, Lucas left a message for the detective in charge of Mi's case and asked him to meet them at her house in the morning. The breaking and entering would have to be documented. Lucas hoped the cameras would lead them to whoever installed them. But he doubted it. The guy who had hooked them up was a pro. It wasn't likely he'd leave a trail leading back to him.

When Mi came out of the closet, Lucas helped her

pack her things. They barely spoke. Lucas waited until they climbed into his car to break the silence.

He shoved the key in the ignition and turned to her. "Who's Jay?"

She flinched. He could see that much in the weak light that filtered into the truck from the streetlights.

"I heard you say his name just before I knocked on your door. Who is he, Mi?"

"You were eavesdropping on me?"

"Your door is as thin as paper." He wasn't going to defend himself or apologize. And he wasn't going to ask her again. They'd sit in the truck all night until she gave him an answer.

"I didn't say Jay, I said Jas for Jason, my brother." Her response reverberated off the window where she'd fixed her attention.

In the dark interior of the truck, Lucas couldn't be sure of the veracity of her answer, but something told him it wasn't a lie. There'd been a note in the file about a brother named Jason. He wrenched the key in the ignition, pretty sure the something that made him want to believe her was his overactive libido as the scent of her filled the confined space and twined around him as her limbs had when they'd kissed. He stared out the windshield into the black night, his eyes adjusting to the darkness, automatically searching the shadows for anything out of the ordinary.

He reminded himself that they'd only met that morning. Hard to believe with all they'd shared. When he'd woken up this morning the name Miyuki Price-Jones had been nothing more than a name on a folder and his chance to even things up with Cal. Now, knowing what she smelled like fresh from her shower, how the hot water gave her skin a delicate blush, and how soft the damp strands of her hair felt against his face, she was more. Much more. And with the hope that she could continue to be more, sprouting and snaking through him like a vine, he had to be sure of her honesty beyond any shadow of a doubt.

Mi stared out the window of Lucas's truck, trying to remember what it had been like to feel safe. Had it only been that morning she'd made plans with Lucy to go to the antique swap meet, hoping she'd find just the right picture for her dining room? And now she was fleeing her home, her landing place when things with her mother got too crazy.

She tried not to think about all of the things she'd sacrificed to build it. The years of working two and three jobs before she'd gotten lucky and landed the co-hosting job at *Pleasure at Home*. Eating at home instead of going out and counting her pennies until payday, hoping she had enough for gas *and* groceries. The personal relationships she hadn't had the time or energy for. Having to buy used cars instead of new. The vacations spent with her mother instead of baking on a warm sandy beach with friends. She'd never even been more than a hundred miles from Dallas in her whole life.

"Mi, look at me," Lucas whispered, his tone gentle and coxing.

She had a right to be mad at him for listening in on her conversation with Jason, but with everything else going on in her life she just didn't have any room inside her for another useless emotion. She gave up the wishing and hoping that this was all a bad dream or a joke and turned away from the house that didn't feel like hers anymore, turning toward Lucas.

"I'm going to need you to be honest with me, Mi. We're partners in this, but if I don't know all of the players I can't do my job. Can you do that?"

She nodded, unable to pull off more than that.

He looked out over the hood of the truck, then back at her. The thin light coming into the truck reflected in his dark eyes, like two lighthouses on a distant shore. She had the feeling he was weighing his next words carefully and that her response would be important to him.

"I saw the baby pictures and bed in the spare bedroom. And the child car seat in your car—"

She answered the question before he could ask it. She'd been expecting it. It wasn't the first time she'd been asked and it wouldn't be the last. "I don't have a baby. I like to go to swap meets and garage sales."

"You buy baby things?" He had that look men get when the words baby and marriage are mentioned.

"Lucy's having a baby."

"Oh. Right." He searched her face in that probing way he had, as if he could read her thoughts. He must have come to some kind of conclusion about her because he nodded, giving her one of his rare smiles, this one was meant to be reassuring. "Sorry. Had to ask. A baby would complicate things."

Mi let out a relieved breath and turned back toward

the window, resting her chin on her fist. "Don't worry about it."

He flipped the headlights on, shifted the truck into gear, and pulled away from her house. "It's going to be all right, you know. You're going to be all right. Do you trust me?"

She glanced at his profile so hard yet noble. Did she trust him? Did she have any other choice? "Where are we going?"

"My place. I have a spare bedroom." He shot her a quick glance when she didn't respond right away. "It's the safest place I could think of."

"Okay."

Out of the corner of her eye, she saw him check on her again, gauging her level of consent. "Unless you have somewhere else you'd rather go."

"Your place is fine, I'm sure. I'm just very tired."

While Lucas took the return call of the detective in charge of her case, Mi sat back in the plush leather seat and replayed her conversation with Lucas, hoping her answers had been enough to assuage his curiosity. She doubted it. Panic clawed at her and she bit down hard on her lip, pushing the fear and dread down. She'd had to structure her life around the terrible decision she'd been forced to make when she was only fifteen. And now she sat in the plush interior, driving who knows where with a man who saw more than he should.

All of her years of careful planning and sacrificing could come crashing down around her with one slip up. She'd be wise to keep her distance from Lucas. He wasn't going to stop asking questions and seeing more than she wanted to show. Suddenly the big man sitting across the darkened cab who touched her so tenderly, kissed her as though he never wanted to stop, and made her want to bare her soul and turn over her troubles to him seemed a bigger threat than the letters, stalker, and cameras combined.

How could she reach out for what Lucas offered when her hands were so full with the barely pasted together shards of her life?

3

Mi hadn't thought about what she expected Lucas's home to be like, but if she had she never would have come up with this gleaming tower situated in heart of the Dallas Arts District. How shabby her tiny little house must have seemed to him by comparison. She wondered why a man who lived like this would take a job as a body-guard. He surely didn't need the money unless guarding people paid more than she thought. *A lot more.*

Lucas pressed a button on the remote hooked to his visor, opening the gate to the underground garage. He rolled the truck through and parked in a reserved space near the glass doors to the lobby. In moments he was ushering Mi into an elevator as he waved to the three doormen manning the security desk. As the elevator door whooshed closed she caught one of the guards eyeing her as though she were a dirty mutt Lucas was smuggling into the building.

She shouldn't be here. This was wrong. She should have insisted on a hotel even though she couldn't afford the expense. She crossed her arms over her chest, catching sight of her reflection in the tinted glass doors. Nervous laughter threatened to bubble up at the mirrored image of her and Lucas standing side by side until she raised her gaze meeting his in their reflection. He was watching her, gauging her reaction. But there was something altogether hot and aching behind his appraisal of her, as though he both longed for and dreaded having her in his home.

Maybe she shouldn't have trusted him so much, allowed him to take control. Chills skittered through her and she rubbed her arms, feeling a bit like the fly to his spider.

Then the doors slid open and the image was gone, replaced by the most plush, modern space she'd ever seen. And beyond that, floor to ceiling glass walls presented a panoramic view of downtown Dallas. Lights twinkled in the distance for miles. Lucas motioned for her to precede him into the apartment... or penthouse. Mi couldn't be sure, but she had a feeling Lucas wouldn't have settled for anything less, which made her wonder about his apparent interest in her.

The thick carpet cushioned their footfalls, creating an eerie hush. Everything was so neat, so polished and new, but impersonal as though anyone could walk into the space and call it their own. Mi wondered how a person could live in a space devoid of personality. A part of her felt sorry for Lucas this beautiful condo was where a person stayed not lived.

"Are you hungry?" he asked.

Mi thought Lucas had loomed large in her small house, but here in this vast space he seemed even larger somehow.

"I don't have much in the fridge, but there's an all night deli around the corner that delivers."

Mi shook her head, scanning the room, trying to take it all in and make it fit with what she knew of Lucas. Or what little she knew of him.

As though reading her thoughts, Lucas filled in the missing pieces. "My ex-girlfriend picked out this apartment and furniture. I like it. Or I did." His gaze roamed the room as hers had. "It's a lot for one person." He shrugged. "I didn't know what to do with it, you know, after." His eyes met hers and the room seemed to shrink, bringing him closer.

"It's... nice."

He let out a harsh laugh. "It's cold."

She didn't think he was only talking about the decor, but the woman who'd chosen it. Curiosity unfurled within her, mingling with jealousy and a teeny tiny seed of resentment. Who was this woman Lucas had trusted with more than just his wallet? Mi looked around again, viewing the space anew. It *was* cold. She suppressed a shudder and turned back to Lucas to find him watching her, waiting for her pronouncement.

"It's modern," she offered.

"You're being nice. The first time I sat on that couch." He pointed to a sharp-angled, leather and steel grouping. "I thought I'd impale myself."

"That could be dangerous. Why do you keep it?"

He hitched a shoulder. "Haven't gotten around to replacing it."

Mi wandered over to the window and looked out. Forty-two floors was a long way up... or down, depending on your perspective. Lucas came up behind her, but didn't touch her. Warmth radiated off him and into her.

"I bought the place for the view." His voice lowered, sending a deep rumbling through her. He was so *close*.

"It's beautiful." Her words came out breathless, almost sultry.

He traced a finger down the side of her throat. "Hmm, it is."

She had a sudden vision of him pressing her against the glass, lifting her skirt and tracing kisses along the line his finger had drawn. He'd take her hard and fast, right there while the whole city watched, her palms sliding down the panes. She swallowed hard, fighting back the urge to lift her skirt for him and beg him to do it. She wanted to lose herself in the mindless give and take, the blinding, driving need. For just a moment, she wanted something for her. To come apart in arms that would support her when she came back together, back to herself.

She took a sliding step to the side and spun away from him. This was not for her. He was not for her. She had to remind herself that this man was a stranger, paid to protect her and nothing more.

"You must be tired." She could hear the rejection in

his voice as though he might have been having similar thoughts.

She cleared her throat, hoping to clear away the need that threatened to swallow her whole. "It is late. And I have a show tomorrow."

"Of course. I'll take you to your room." He grabbed her bag from the chair where he'd dropped it earlier and proceeded down the hall to the right.

Mi followed him past two doors to a set of double doors. Lucas opened one, not stopping to see if she followed. The bedroom was nearly as large as the living room with two full walls of windows in an L shape. The large bed sat on a platform positioned for a perfect view of the Dallas skyline.

Lucas sat her bag on the bed, then disappeared through yet another door. Mi followed, stopping short at the entrance to a closet. Shirts, jackets, trousers, and suits lined the walls broken only by a bank of drawers and a section of tilted shelves that displayed shoes of every kind.

"This is your room."

Lucas continued to go through drawers, pulling clothing out. "Yes."

"I can't... that is... you don't expect..."

Lucas looked up from his task, then in two steps he was standing in front of her. She almost backed away on instinct. He placed a hand on the doorway above her head and bent down to her.

His gaze pinned her in place, his words flowing over her like warm honey. "No, I don't expect." His voice dropped to a whisper that stroked her senses as if he'd touched her. "I want."

Heat shot straight through her and with nothing more than his words she was wet and pulsing with need for him. Her nipples chapped against the fabric of her shirt, heightening her excitement. She pressed her legs together, holding in the sensation.

He leaned down and placed a gentle kiss at the corner of her mouth. "But not tonight." He pushed off the doorframe and went back to his task, collecting what he needed.

"But this is your room," she whispered, not trusting her full voice.

"And the one furthest from the front door. I need to be between you and whatever may come." He gathered the pile he'd assembled and came toward her, backing her into the bedroom.

She followed him back down the hall, curious to see where he'd go. Not that she cared. She really shouldn't care. It was just that she needed to know where he was in case of whatever might come. At least that's what she told herself. He went into the room closest to the living area and furthest from his bedroom. Another wall of windows spanned this bedroom, a guest room from the look of it.

Lucas set his things on the dresser and turned to her. "Are you sure you're not hungry?"

"No." Not for food anyway.

"Then off to bed with you."

He gripped her by the shoulders, spun her around, and marched her back down the hall to his bedroom.

At the door he moved his hands up, cupping her face, his fingers tangling in her hair. Then with his eyes on hers he bent down and gave her the most chaste goodnight kiss, the first date kind.

"Goodnight, *querida*." He closed the door with a quiet snick, leaving a void of warmth in his wake.

Mi leaned against the door, pressing her face to the paneled wood, and smoothed her hands over it, as she would like to have touched him. When he was there she felt safe and overwhelmed all at once. With him gone the room felt vast and empty. *She* felt empty. Mi wrenched herself from the door, feeling silly and lonely, and forced herself to go through the routine of getting ready for bed. It was nearly midnight, but she wasn't tired. After brushing her teeth and changing into a nightgown she examined the bed, certain she'd need to take a running jump at it.

Instead she went to the closet. The light flickered on automatically revealing a neatness that bordered on military precision. Each hanger was spaced equal distance from the other, the shoes rivaled a store display, and there wasn't a speck of dust or stray sock to be found. She wondered if he'd notice if she changed things around or moved a few hangers so their spacing was more random. Once the thought struck, she couldn't get it out of her head. She tapped a hanger closer to its neighbor, then switched two of the shirts. Smiling to herself, she felt oddly relieved as though she and Lucas were now on a more even keel. He needed a little chaos in his life. Lord knew she had that in abundance.

Mi wandered back into the bedroom and turned out the lights. The skyline illuminated the room, lengthening the shadows, lending a coolness to the space that would have been romantic if she had someone to share it with. She climbed into the bed and settled amongst the pillows. Sleep eluded her, her thoughts jumbling and crashing into each other, replaying scenes from the day over and over.

After a half hour she gave up and padded out into the living space, looking for the kitchen and hopefully a glass of warm milk. She stopped when she heard Lucas murmuring, then tip-toed further down the hall until she could see him sitting on the floor in front of the sharp-looking sofa group. He faced the window, his back to her. She thought he might be on the phone and turned to go back to her bedroom when his voice startled her.

"Can't sleep, *querida*?"

The man had supernatural hearing. Mi inched her way into the room, stopping when the sofa blocked her way.

Lucas looked over his shoulder at her. "Come here. There's someone I want you to meet."

Mi didn't know what to expect so when she caught sight of the small fluff of orange fur cupped in his large hands, she gasped and rushed over for a closer look.

Lucas held his hands out to her. "Want to hold him?"

Dropping to her knees, Mi looked into the bright blue eyes of the little orange kitten and her heart melted. She scooped him out of Lucas's hands. "Oh!

He's purring." She hugged the kitten close to her body. Gently stroking his head, she marveled at how soft his fur was.

If Lucas had known what kind of miracle Mi's smile was, he would have carried a dozen kittens in his pockets just to see it every day. She looked up at him with the most amazing expression, her amber eyes crinkling at the corners. His heart did a slow roll in his chest and he swallowed hard, his palms growing damp. If he'd thought her pretty before, he was wrong. When she truly smiled, she was luminous. The simple joy of holding a kitten radiated from her into him and he felt like a teenager on the verge of his first kiss.

"Where'd you get him?" Mi asked, cradling the kitten against her chest.

"Found him on the side of the road a couple of blocks away."

"A stray. You poor thing." She snuggled the cat closer. "What's his name?"

Lucas would have given anything to trade places with that cat and felt a bit stupid for having the thought. "Gooch," he answered.

Mi's brows dipped. "Why did you name him Gooch?"

"He reminds me of a friend I had."

"You had a friend named *Gooch*?"

"It was what everyone called him."

"Why does he remind you of your friend?"

Lucas took the opportunity to scoot closer to Mi, stroking a finger over the kitten's head and down his back. "Gooch had orange hair that stuck up all over his head when it grew long and huge blue eyes." Lucas chuckled at the memory that still carried the pang of loss. "His eyes were so big and round they looked like marbles. Just like this guy's."

"What happened to him?" Mi asked her tone hushed as if she was afraid to tread on bad memories.

"He was killed during the same mission that earned me a ticket home."

"I'm sorry."

"Me too."

"What happened?"

Lucas looked away and out into the night as if the lights that twinkled back at him could relieve the misery of that night a year ago. "He took a bullet meant for me." There was more, the blood flowing over his hands as he held the pieces of his friend's skull together. The tufts of orange hair matted with blood and brain matter. And the blank, far-away look in those big, too fucking trusting, blue eyes.

"I'm so, so sorry."

Lucas looked down at Mi's hand gripping his forearm, then up into golden eyes wide with sympathy and something more... understanding maybe. She'd known loss. He could see it in the honest way she looked at him. Knowing they shared that, gave him more comfort than her words. If she had been anyone else he would have brushed her off with something glib like *It was a long time ago*, but that wouldn't be fair to either of them.

"I miss him," he said simply, reaching out to stroke the cat again.

She didn't comment, just let the words hang in the

air between them. The silence she lent him soaked up some of the grief. She didn't give him platitudes or try to tell him it was God's way or some other kind of bull-shit like that. She let him have the moment to miss his friend.

Mi smoothed her hand away, her attention once again on the kitten. "I knew you'd been in the military. What branch?"

"Navy. SEALS."

"Huh, I would have figured you for a Marine."

"Those girls?"

"My father was a Marine."

"Damn," Lucas said. "Sorry. No offense to your father."

Mi laughed and Lucas thought it was the most incredible sound he'd ever heard. He felt a little bit light headed when he was with her, as though the air was somehow thinner in the space around her.

"None taken," she replied.

"Where does he live, your father?"

"He died when I was two."

"Now I'm sorry."

"Don't be."

She shrugged it off, but Lucas felt her decades old pain as if it was his own. He wanted to reach out, touch her, but she'd tucked herself up tight. Her legs bent under her, her arms close to her body.

She sighed and bent her head towards the kitten. "I look like my father, I think. He named me after his Japanese mother."

"I'd wondered about that. And Price-Jones?"

"Welsh. On his father's side."

"What about your mother?" Lucas asked.

Mi shifted and if he hadn't been watching her so closely he might have missed the look of regret that flashed across her face. "She lives in Garland."

"Any other siblings besides your brother Jason?"

"I think he's asleep."

Lucas looked down at the kitten curled up her hands. He let her change the subject and gazed out at the skyline, content just to be near her.

Mi adjusted her position, drawing his attention back to her. She sat Indian-style, pulling her plain cotton nightgown over her knees, creating a cradle in the hollow between her legs for the kitten. When she'd settled him she met Lucas's gaze and gave him a small smile.

"How'd you go from being a Navy SEAL to being a bodyguard?"

Lucas rubbed his thigh, extending his legs out in front of him, his bare feet pressing against the window. If he leaned a little closer to her it was no accident. "I didn't. I'm not."

She pulled back a little, frowning. "Then what's this?"

"I'm doing a favor for Cal while I'm between jobs."

"What do you mean a favor?"

Lucas stretched his arms out across the seat of the sofa. He lifted the ends of Mi's hair between his fingers, mesmerized by its softness. "I owed Cal a favor and had the skill set to do the job so I took it."

"Must have been a huge debt you owed."

"It was."

She looked as though she'd inquire further, then changed her mind, gazing out at the view. He watched her, absorbing everything about her. The scent of her, lighter now, but still hers. The way her nightgown dipped down between her breasts, the thin cotton clinging to her hardened nipples. The red painted toes peeking out from beneath her knees. The way she absently petted the kitten as she looked out into the night. He wanted to touch her, bring her attention back to him. But then he wouldn't be so free to let his gaze roam over her.

"I've heard it before, but what does *querida* mean?"

He hadn't realized she'd turned her head to look at him. He'd been so focused on her breasts poking against the fabric of her gown, wondering if she was cold or something more.

"Darling, dear, beloved," he answered softly.

Her eyes grew wider, darker and her tongue swept across her bottom lip. "Oh."

He brought the hand that had been playing with her hair up to her nape, cradling the back of her head in his hand. Bringing her closer, he leaned down, his focus on her lips and the way they parted, inviting him. She tilted her face up to his, a further invitation. And that was all he needed. As their lips met, he thrilled with the satisfaction that she could be his.

She moaned, winding her arms around his neck, her fingers threading through the hair at his nape. His other hand went to her knee, the thin cotton covering it was no barrier for him. In a flash, he slipped beneath it to the smooth skin of her thigh. He explored her mouth, tracing his tongue over her lips, dipping inside. She let out a soft sound of pleasure when he sucked on her lower lip, his hand at the curving the underside of her breast.

He cupped her breast, so small and firm, her nipple pressing into his palm. Her hand had found its way under his t-shirt and he'd thought he'd die with need for the feel of her hands on him. He left her mouth, nibbling and kissing a path down her neck. He hooked a finger, then another into the neckline of her night-gown, pulling it down. She arched into his caress, lifting up onto her knees.

"Meow."

She jerked away from him, reaching for the kitten she'd dislodged from her lap. His fingers lost their grip and he watched in shock as her nipple disappeared back down the neckline of her gown. He'd been millimeters from having it in his mouth.

Damned cat.

"Oh, Gooch. You poor thing." She examined the kitten, lifting it up. "You could have been crushed."

"He'll live."

She settled the kitten in her lap again. "Have you taken him to the vet? He might have fleas and he'll need shots."

"I know."

"Where does he sleep?"

"I have a box for him in the laundry room."

She looked at him as if he put the cat to bed dangling at the end of a fishing pole out the window.

"What?" he asked.

"You make him sleep *alone*?"

He didn't have a coherent response for that. He figured it was probably a trick question anyway so even if he could come up with an answer it would be akin to *Why yes, those pants* do *make your ass look huge.* But then he looked down into those amazing golden eyes and grew stupid enough to say, "He can sleep with you tonight."

"Really?" Holding the kitten, she bounced up to her knees. She put a hand on his shoulder and leaned in, dropping a kiss on his cheek. "Thank you." Before he could get a hold of her, she was on her feet, walking away. "Goodnight." She snuggled the kitten to her neck, murmuring to it as she disappeared down the hall.

He glanced down at the raging hard-on straining against his shorts. Fucking Gooch always did get the girl.

THE FOLLOWING MORNING Lucas and Mi met the detective in charge of her case at Mi's house. She wanted to stay in the truck, but Lucas wouldn't let her. Following him and the lead detective into her house, loneliness crept over her, leaving her oddly bereft. Her little neighborhood had gone through a transformation, changing from a place she felt safe to a place that had let her down. Mrs. Wickerson peeped through her drapes across the street just as she always did when anything bigger than the Stanton's Chihuahua stepped foot on the street. Where was her nosy neighbor when that creep had installed cameras in her house?

Lucas took Detective Rolls through the house to her bedroom to show him the cameras he'd found. The detective seemed to defer to Lucas and his knowledge of covert surveillance from the moment he'd stepped foot in the house. Plainly showing how impressed he was, Rolls asked question after question. The steady flow of them reached Mi in the entryway.

Mi stood in the foyer of the house she'd been so proud of, feeling it had somehow betrayed her. Somebody had been watching her in her most private moments. Tears pricked the back of her eyes and she swallowed hard, pushing back the sob that crept up her throat. Rubbing her arms, she shuddered. She heard Lucas and the detective coming back down the hall. Dropping her arms and standing up straighter, she pasted on a brave face.

"I'll need a team to go through the place. That'll take some time, ya know." Detective Rolls turned his fat wrist, glancing at the watch straining against his flesh. "Couple hours or so. You got somewhere to be?"

"I have to be at work by ten," Mi said.

"Work," Rolls snorted as he shook his head, his jowls flapping, like a hound dog. "Jesus H. Christmas just when I'd thought I'd seen it all." He gave Lucas a jab with his elbow. "You seen what they do there for profit?" He didn't wait for a response. "Now I ain't one to judge, mind you. What two reasonably mature people do in the privacy of the boudoir and all sure ain't my business. But it just seems so unseemly, all them fake wieners lyin' about. And then those other things." He waved a meaty hand around. "Whatchya call 'em? Them things with the holes for the men?"

"Strokers," Mi provided.

"Strokers. Jesus H. Christmas. Don't need to waste my money when I got Rosie and her five sisters right here." He put his hand up and wiggled his sausage fingers. "If you catch my meanin'." He winked and prodded Lucas with his elbow again.

Mi rolled her lips under, suppressing a smile. She'd come across Detective Rolls's type before. They were relatively harmless, seeing what Mi did as a novelty. It was the others, the ones who didn't think what she did was fun or entertaining who were the dangerous ones. People like Cookie Dixon and the members of C.A.L.M.

Lucas cleared his throat. His brows nearly touching over the bridge of his nose, his mouth pressed into a grim line, the glare he gave Rolls was hard-edged reproof. He waited until the other man subsided, visually shrinking under Lucas's stare. "I'm guessing you'll find a camera either outside over the front door or over there." Lucas pointed to the sliding glass door that lead out to the small backyard. "He'd want to see her enter."

Rolls gave Lucas an assessing look, his florid face bunching up around his eyes. "Uh, huh. And just howd'ya figure that?"

"It's what I'd do."

"That so. What else wouldya do?"

"I'd want an eye in every room."

Lucas seemed to settle into the roll of expert as he walked Rolls through the living areas, pointing out the best possible vantage point for each camera. Mi wasn't sure she liked this side of Lucas. It brought him in line with the man who'd invaded her home, her privacy. Mi moved to the door, shivering. She wanted out, away.

"Ah, damn." Lucas came to her and rubbed her arms. "Sorry. Do you want wait in the bedroom while we talk?"

She shook her head. She didn't want to be in there alone. She just wanted to be far, far away. "No. I'm fine." She waved him off with false reassurance. "Go ahead."

Lucas looked as though he wanted to call a halt to the whole thing and maybe whisk her off until Rolls drew his attention away.

"What about at night? Wouldya need night vision?"

Lucas gave her a half smile that didn't reach his eyes and her arms a gentle squeeze. "We won't be much longer." He turned to Rolls. "And motion detection. I'd want ears, too, but then I'm greedy."

Lucas really seemed to be in his element. Mi was glad to have him on her side.

"*That* would cost ya." Rolls draped an arm across his belly and propped his elbow in his hand while he stroked his chin, considering. "There's a factor to keep in mind. Whoever did this had some bank. Or access to."

"I'd be surprised if you found more than basic motion activated cameras. But if you do, would you let me know?"

"I could do that. I bet you have some stories to tell." Rolls nudged him with his elbow again. "I was an Army man myself. Got me an in with the force, but then that was before all that Post Traumatic B.S."

"Uh, huh." Lucas's brow buckled in a deep frown. "An associate of mine is on his way over. He'll lock up when your guys are finished."

"Ah, here's the tech boys now," Rolls said, moseying to the screen door to let them in.

Lucas and Mi waited while Rolls directed his team. When he'd finished, Lucas handed over the letters from Doyle Gann, explaining what the convict's last letter contained.

Rolls snorted. "Revolvin' doors, that's all prisons are these days. I'll contact his parole officer." He waved the plastic bag with the letter. "This'll get him revoked, I'm sure. Don't cha worry miss, we'll get 'im."

She sincerely hoped that was true. "Thank you, Detective."

Lucas led Mi out of the house and into the hard baked sunshine. Heat waves shimmered above the pavement and the air closed in around them, like a stifling embrace. A sleek red car pulled up across the street and a tall, lean black man emerged, his eyes covered with mirrored aviator glasses. Mi watched him cross the street with an ambling gate, all loose limbs and confidence.

"Malcolm, thanks for coming." The men performed a combination handshake/half-hug greeting. Lucas turned to her. "Mi meet Malcolm Oubre. Malcolm, Miyuki Price-Jones."

Malcolm whipped off his glasses, revealing startling turquoise eyes. He bent over Mi's hand, his deep baritone vibrating her chest. "Miss Price-Jones, a pleasure."

Mi couldn't help it. She blushed, her other hand fluttering over her breasts. Such charm should be bottled and sold with a warning label. "Pleased to meet you, too, Malcolm. Please, call me Mi."

Lucas shifted behind her a fraction, swelling up to his full height. He leaned in, crowding Malcolm out. She felt the heat from his wide palm low on her back like a brand.

Malcolm straightened and donned his glasses, his wide, white-toothed smile never wavering. "Oh, I always aim to please, Miss Mi. *Always*."

Mi resisted the urge to fan herself. She was surely buying whatever it was Malcolm was selling, as Lucy would say. "I'm sure you do."

"If you're finished," Lucas said to Malcolm, disapproval sharpening each word. "I'll introduce you to the detective in charge so you can get to the job you came here to do."

Mi followed them back into the house, going no further inside than the foyer. In a moment Lucas came back down the hall, gripped her elbow and led her back outside to his truck. She had to jog a little to keep up with him. He opened the car door, wrapped his hands around her waist and hoisted her up on the seat before she knew what was happening. She began to say something about Lucas's strong reaction, but the door shut abruptly, leaving her open mouthed and sputtering.

Lucas climbed into the truck and turned the key

with more force than necessary. She'd just barely clicked on her seatbelt when the truck shot away from the curb, knocking her back against the seat. She angled herself to glare up at him, preparing to unleash her temper, but one look at his at his face stopped her before the words could form.

"You're grinning." Her bubble of annoyance evaporated into disbelief. She gaped at him, sure she was stuck in the cab of the truck with a lunatic.

"You should have seen yourself."

"What?"

"Malcolm." He shook his head, his smile spreading, crinkling the corners of his eyes. "I don't know how he does it."

"What?"

They'd stopped at a light and he turned to her, his dark eyes glinting in the morning light, like the gleam of sunlight off deep water. "I wish I could do that. Just once. That man could charm the panties off a superfluity of nuns."

"A what of what?"

He smacked the steering wheel with the palm of his hand. "And when he pulled his shades down... the look on your face." He chuckled, letting her in on the joke.

A smile tipped up one corner of her lips. "He is good."

"It's a damn shame his door doesn't swing that way." Lucas shook his head sadly. "Such a waste."

"How do you know him?"

"Navy. We were on the same team until he got out two years ago."

"What about 'Don't Ask, Don't Tell'?"

He hitched a shoulder. "No one asked, no one told, but everyone knew. Didn't matter with Malcolm. Everyone wanted to be his wing-man."

"I bet. What does he do for a living?"

"Private Investigator."

They turned into the industrial complex, then made a right turn headed toward the *Pleasure at Home* studio. They could see the crowd already gathered at the gates, banners and picket signs in use. The smiles slid from their faces, their moment of levity crushed under the weight of reality. Lucas sat up straighter in his seat, signaling his shift into the role of bodyguard. Mi wrapped her arms around herself and slunk down in her seat, resenting her role of hapless victim.

Lucas glanced over at Mi's pale face, hating the hunted look in her eyes. He clicked her seatbelt open. "Get down into the foot well. Stay down until I tell you to get up."

As they neared the gate, the crowd's attention switched from Cookie Dixon and the man standing next to her on the makeshift dais to the truck coming toward them. The chanting increased at the sight of the new target. They closed in, surrounding the truck, making it difficult to move more than a few inches at a time toward the gate.

Lucas laid on the horn, taking satisfaction in making a few of the protesters start at the sound. Fists pounded the truck's exterior as it inched past. They were fully surrounded now. Lucas resisted the urge to jam down on the accelerator. Narrowly. He hit the horn again, then just leaned against it, drowning out all but the closest voices. Faces pressed against the windows briefly before sliding away with the truck's movement. He hoped to God they would only see him in the cab and not Mi.

Cookie Dixon sneered down from her perch, shouting into her megaphone. Her face reddened with the effort to be heard. The man beside her looked on, watching as though he was memorizing the truck and driver. Lucas made a mental note to find out who that guy was. Something about the way he stood, separate but interested, made the fine hairs on Lucas's neck stand on end. He never ignored his instinct.

4

The mob broke, parting at the property line of the *Pleasure at Home* studio, allowing Lucas to enter. He hit the gas pedal, eager to put the noise and anger behind them. Mi seemed to sense the danger had passed and inched up into the seat. She kneeled, leaning over the back of the seat, looking out the darkly tinted back window, her ass nearly eye level. Lucas narrowly avoided plowing into a parked car. The spike of adrenaline apparently had no dampening effect on his ability to appreciate her ass. And what a sweet little ass it was, snug in tight denim.

He rolled the truck around the corner of the building and into a parking space out of sight from the entrance. Mi dropped down into the seat and sighed, leaning back to look at him.

"Are you all right?" he asked, taking her in from head to toe. She didn't look any worse for wear other than the lip she chewed on. "Hey." He reached out and ran a fingertip over her worn lip. "None of that. You're fine. I've got you."

She rubbed her lips together, then relaxed enough to give him a small smile. He felt like a conquering hero.

"It's a lot easier to run the gauntlet in your truck than in my compact." She glanced over her shoulder as though she could see the crowd gathered on the other side of the building. "I wish they'd understand what I do. What *good* we do with the show. But all they see is perversion."

"Not everyone is as comfortable with the idea of using... ah, marital aids as you are. Maybe they think it's like bringing a cannon to a gunfight. Awkward and completely unnecessary."

She considered him for a moment with a small frown between her brows. The longer she focused on him the more uncomfortable he became until he burst out of the truck and stalked around to her side.

"Idiot," he muttered to himself.

He helped her slide down from the truck, then stepped back to enjoy the view of her bending over to grab her bag from the floor board. He shoved his hands in his pockets to keep from giving her a pat or grope. They walked to the employee entrance of the studio side by side in silence. He strode with his shoulders hunched, hoping she'd let his remark slide by without comment.

Just as he reached for the door handle, she snatched that chance away. "You're uncomfortable with what I do." She said it as though she was reconsidering everything she'd ever thought about him. And not in a good way.

He hitched up his shoulders in a helpless shrug. "It's unusual."

She shifted back, parking a hand on her hip. "It embarrasses you. *I* embarrass you."

"No. It's not... that is... You don't embarrass me." He reached for the door handle again. "You're gonna be late."

She slapped a palm on the door and leaned all her body weight into it, preventing him from opening it. He gripped the handle, struggling with her for a moment before giving up. If he used anymore strength he'd send her backwards onto her sweet little ass.

"Have you ever used toys in the bedroom? Maybe a pair of fuzzy handcuffs or stimulating lubricant?" She tossed that out as though she were asking him if he'd ever used deodorant or put sheets on his bed. Ordinary things everyone used. She scanned his face for a response, but he did his best to keep it carefully blank. "Colored condoms? Flavored lotions? Massage oils?" Her face slowly changed with each question, like the first rays of sunrise moving over the land, from curiosity to disbelief to outright astonishment. "Wow," she said on an exhaled breath, then swallowed hard.

She made him seem like some kind of freak and then it dawned on him that she'd probably experimented with all of those things and more. Defensive anger backed up in his chest, hurting a little, and he stared at her hard. She flinched and took a half step back. He tried to soften his expression, but couldn't quite manage it with the images his mind put before him of her and any number of men performing all kinds of kinky sex acts.

She risked one more question. "Have you ever wanted to?"

"No."

"Oh." She looked deeply disappointed. In him? In herself? She shifted her bag on her shoulder and kept her gaze straight ahead, hitting him just below his chest. "I do," she whispered.

"Do what?"

"Want to try those things."

"You mean you've never...?"

She shook her head. "Never mind." She reached for the door handle and this time it was he who put out his palm to stop it.

They didn't speak for a long moment. He stared at her bent head, trying to wrap his mind around what she'd said and not said. His chest swelled at the implication of her words. She wanted to try all of those things and maybe more. With him.

Wanting confirmation of his thoughts, he lifted her chin with the crook of his finger. She kept her eyes cast down as he slowly raised her face up to his and then they flew open wide. What he saw in their deep golden depth was defiance tinged with uncertainty and mortification. And what always seemed to happen when he looked into her eyes happened again. His thoughts slowed, his stomach felt nervous to the point of nausea, his mouth dried up, and his heart beat in a hard thumping rhythm. When she looked at him like that, he wanted to give her whatever she asked for.

He opened his mouth to tell her just this, but before he could get the words out a car came around the corner of the building, startling them both. Lucas moved faster than Mi could blink, shoving her behind him. He had his gun drawn before either of them registered whose car it was. The sleek silver Mercedes Benz CL600 Coupe slid into the specially designated spot closest to the door. The driver opened the car door and slowly unfolded his tall frame with the ease of a man who held power like a dog on a chain. His golden head bent down to receive his buff colored Stetson, shielding his face from their view.

Hat firmly in place, Cal Sellers raised his head, flashing Mi and Lucas the smile that closed a thousand deals a day. He presented a picture, stretching an arm across the roof of his car, holding the door in the other hand for a moment as though he had all the leisure time in the world. Or was posing for a business magazine spread.

Lucas slid his gun back into his waistband.

"Honey, come on out and meet my friends," he said, then closed the door and made his way toward Lucas and Mi, leaving 'Honey' to scamper out her side of the car on her own.

While Cal and Lucas greeted each other with a handshake and slaps on the arms, Mi watched as 'Honey' picked her way across the pitted parking lot in the short steps her skin-tight suit would allow. Mi worried for her. Between her over-inflated breasts that looked like they played hell with her balance and the sky-high shoes with spiked heels, Mi was sure 'Honey' would turn an ankle or worse.

Cal always had a 'Honey' with him, acting as his assistant. Mi wasn't sure why a businessman would need a woman like that following him around all day. She figured maybe she was a status symbol like his Mercedes and Rolex. An accessory that reflected his wealth and success.

Cal greeted Mi, bending his lean frame to scoop her up in a warm embrace. "How's my little star? I swear, darlin', you get prettier and prettier every time I see you." He winked at her, all good ole boy charm and wolf smile. He tipped his head toward Lucas. "I see this big block has been doing his job, keeping you safe. Don't let his good looks fool you, darlin'. This one's a killer. I'd trust him to guard my own dear mother. You're as safe as Fort Knox."

Slinging an arm across their shoulders, Cal rounded up Mi and Lucas and herded them through the door into the busy studio, keeping up an effusive dialog that was short on information and long on BS. 'Honey' trotted to keep up after them. Cal's presence had a rippling effect on the employees of *Pleasure at Home*. Everyone dropped what they were doing and came over to greet him like the golden boy come home.

Crosby marched to the front of the line and stuck his hand out to his boss. "Mr. Sellers, good of you to visit." They shook hands. "I hope you're staying for the taping. The folks in marketing put together a terrific lineup for tonight. Some of our top selling products."

Without taking his focus off Cal's face, Crosby said, "You've got ten minutes for makeup, Mi, then I want you on set."

"Yes, Crosby." Mi got a pat on the back from Cal as he released her. Lucas trailed on her heels, which she hadn't expected. "I'm just going to makeup. I'll be right out."

"I go where you go."

"But Cal—"

"Expects me to do my job not hover around him like one of his honeys. And my job is with you—"

"Yes, I know. Twenty-four seven."

Mi wasn't sure why she was short with him, but it might have had something to do with throwing herself at him, practically begging him to fulfill her fantasies. Fantasies that disgusted and embarrassed him. She could just die. How humiliating! She knew he was about to reject her when Cal had come flying around the corner, distracting him. What an idiot she was. He was here to do a job, nothing more.

She made a vow right then to keep things strictly business between them. It was for the best, she told herself. A complicated man like Lucas would only add to her troubles, not take them away. She sneaked a peek at his profile out of the corner of her eye. But oh, the shivers that raced through her when she did nothing more than look at him. And when he touched her, she burned for him, all of her cares melting away under his dark gaze and heated caress.

Tracey had set out all of the implements of her trade and flitted about, not bothering to hide her impatience with Mi's tardiness. "Thank goodness you're here." She began work on Mi's hair as soon as her bottom hit the chair. "Crosby's been in a snit, checking in with me every other minute to see if you've arrived. If he popped his head in here one more time I was going to make him up in your place."

"Sorry. The protestors gave us a terrible time. I can't believe how many of them there are now."

"I see you brought your boyfriend with you again."

Boyfriend. Mi caught Lucas's reflection in the mirror. His back was to them, but she was sure he could easily hear them in the small space. "Yes."

"*That* must be going well." Tracey bent down to whisper in Mi's ear. "But doesn't he have job? I mean, how does he have the time to hang out here all day? Or can't he bear to part from you?"

Mi didn't like Tracey's tone. It had an edge to it that pricked her anger. Mi balled her fists in her lap out of sight under the counter. She'd always considered Tracey a friend. Could it be her friend was jealous?

"He wanted to see what I do."

Tracey straightened. "Uh-huh."

Mi didn't owe Tracey an explanation. She had a feeling there was no answer she could give that would satisfy Tracey's unexpected bitterness toward Lucas anyway.

In no time Tracey had Mi's hair up in her usual on camera style and was applying Mi's lipstick when Davy poked his head in the door. "I'm sorry, Miz Mi, but Crosby says you've thirty seconds to... and he's making me quote him... 'Get your ass on set before I fire you and you have to get a job swinging a sign dressed like a goddamned sandwich at the mall food court.' Only he said it a lot louder than that so you'd better hurry." He bobbed his head. "Sorry, Miz Mi."

"That's all right, Davy. I'm finished except for my glasses." Mi looked at Tracey. "Where are my glasses?" Mi pointed to a tray on the counter. "I left them right there."

Tracey buckled her brows. "Are you sure that's where you put them?"

"Yes. I put them there after every show. They have to be here somewhere. Help me look."

Mi, Davy, and Tracey searched the small makeup room with no luck.

Using the edge of the counter, Mi climbed to her feet after searching underneath. "I don't understand where they could have gone."

"There's only one pair. What are you going to do?"

Davy backed out of the room. "I'll just go and check on... something." Then he scuttled away as fast as his little bowed legs would take him.

Tracey laughed. "He's making himself scarce for the Crosby explosion."

Mi didn't blame him. This was going to have Crosby hitting his flask again. "Someone had to have taken them," she said to Tracey. "I can't think of any other explanation."

"Who would do that?"

Mi wasn't sure how much Crosby had told the staff about what had been happening, but they had to have noticed. Either way Mi decided it wasn't her call, knowing if she told Tracey it would be like sending a companywide email. "I don't know."

"You know, I think I have to pee." And Tracey backed out of the makeup room, too, leaving Mi to face Crosby alone.

Lucas straightened from his station against the wall and followed Mi as she came out of the makeup room. "Everything all right?"

"No. My glasses are missing."

"You don't have an extra pair?"

"No."

Mi marched up to Crosby, who was deep in conversation with the lighting director. "Excuse me, Crosby, can I speak with you a moment?"

"Only if you're going to tell me you're ready."

"Well—"

"Where are your glasses?"

"They're missing."

Crosby took a deep breath through his nose, pinching the bridge to calm himself, probably for Mr. Sellers's benefit. "Missing."

"Yes."

"Of course they are. Davy!"

"I, ah, think Davy had to go see about something. We looked and looked for them, but they're just gone."

"Gone. Perfect. Ab-so-fucking-lutely perfect. Did you know, Greg here was just telling me that there's a problem with the goddamned lighting?"

"Ah, no."

Crosby made a shooing motion. "Go. Send someone out to buy another pair. No. I want twelve goddamned pairs. I'll lock eleven of them in my goddamned desk drawer so this never happens again!" His voice had gotten progressively louder, ending at his usual shouting level. He turned to Greg the lighting guy. "And you. I want those goddamned lights fixed before Mi's glasses get here. Got it?" He rose from his director's chair and stomped back to his office.

Stepping out of the shadows, Davy reappeared at her side. "I'll go, Miz Mi."

"Thank you, Davy."

"Come with me," Lucas whispered, gripping her elbow and signaling Cal with a tip of his head to follow them.

When they'd all crammed into the makeup room, Lucas asked Cal to close the door behind them.

"Wait for me out here, will ya, Honey?" he told his assistant before she could squeeze herself in, then closed the door. He looked back and forth between Lucas and Mi. "I gather there's a problem."

"You need more security here. Around the clock."

Cal appeared to consider Lucas's words, but underneath Mi could tell he was seething. Cal didn't like to be told what to do. "Explain."

Lucas filled him in on the sabotage, the cameras in Mi's home and the threatening letter from the Doyle Gann. "It's escalating. Two guys walking the perimeter during business hours aren't enough. You need security inside the studio and at the gates, keeping that mob back." And then Lucas said the one thing that was sure to make Cal sit up and take notice. "The sabotage and delays are probably costing you more money than you'd spend."

"I'll take care of it," he said and opened the door. "Honey, I've got some phone calls I want you to make." He looked over his shoulder at Lucas and Mi. "Keep me informed." And then he closed the door behind him.

"I hate thinking one of us is doing this," Mi said. "We're like a family."

"If you had to pick someone, who would you think of first?"

She nibbled her lip, contemplating his question. She'd worked with most of the staff since she started with the show. Imagining one of them turning against the rest was unthinkable. She knew their families, considered them friends.

"Any new employees lately?" he prompted. "Anyone seem unhappy or angry?"

"There's not a high turnover rate. If anyone's unhappy they haven't expressed it to me. I'm sorry. I wish I could be more help."

"How about this: Has anyone gotten religion lately? Shown sudden disapproval over the show's products?"

She considered his question carefully. The only unusual display of disapproval had come from Tracey, but that had been about Lucas, not the show.

"No, not that I know of."

As he took in her words, Mi used his temporary distraction to study him. It wasn't often she got to look at him without his attention on her. His focus on her never wavered, never allowed for this slow perusal without Mi giving away the fact that she was staring, gawking at him like a lovesick teenager. There was a lot to take in.

He'd thrown on dark jeans and a charcoal t-shirt that rode every muscle of his torso and arms like a lover. There was a small mole under his left ear. She hadn't noticed that before. His dark hair curled around the shell of his ear and down his neck. She knew how thick and soft it was, and she had suppressed the urge to reach up and run her fingers through it. The glint of a silver chain winked out at her from just above his collar. She wondered about the significance of the necklace, as he wore no other jewelry.

She didn't dare let her gaze wander farther south. Last night she'd seen the sculpted muscles of his legs, dusted with dark hair. There wasn't one inch of him she'd change. If anything, this moment she'd taken to study him had done her more harm than good. He would play heavily in her fantasies tonight. As he had last night. She sighed. If only she'd been able to slip her vibrator into her overnight bag without Lucas seeing it. The pent up sexual frustration was going to kill her for sure.

Her sigh brought his attention back to her. "Okay. Keep your eyes open for anything. Any difference of attitude, tone, anything out of the ordinary, someone hanging around or being where they shouldn't, stuff like that."

"Sure."

He watched her in that probing way he had for a moment, then moved into her, backing her up against the door. "Are you sure you're all right?" He touched a finger to her lip, tracing it slowly back and forth. "You're doing it again," he whispered, crowding her, his head lowering toward hers.

She put her hands on the hard planes of his chest and gave a shove that didn't budge him. "Don't."

He placed his hands flat on the door, bracketing her head as he pushed back from her, separating their bodies. His dark chocolate gaze locked with hers. "Is it about what I said earlier?"

Again he saw too much. With only inches between them, heat from him radiated into her. She had to fight the urge to wrap herself around him "No. Forget it. Let me out. I've got to go over the products we'll be showcasing tonight."

He traced a finger along her jaw, sending a wicked little shiver through her. "All right, *querida*. We'll talk about this later." He bent and kissed her cheek before reaching for the doorknob. "Until later." He gave her room to leave, holding the door open for her, then followed her out into the studio.

Mi stepped up onto the *Pleasure at Home* set and sat down on the sofa to go over the products she'd be showcasing today. Great. It was couples night. Once a month the show featured products and devices geared toward couples play. After her embarrassing conversation with Lucas, she would have to describe and demonstrate some of the very same products she'd practically begged him to try with her. With him standing just feet away. Watching. Judging.

Mortification burned her cheeks as she stared down at the furry pink handcuffs with matching blindfold, the multi-flavored, stimulating lubricant sampler, and vibrating cock ring. The toys she wanted to try. There were others as well: a non-stinging whip, a sex swing (okay, maybe she wanted to try that one, too), a bridal seduction kit, Thirty-one Favors Body Paint, a card game, toys for same sex couples, and a sensual massage kit, which would be the night's special.

She flipped through the blue cards listing the products and features, jotting notes here and there on some of the descriptions she wanted to be sure to focus on. She always put herself in the role of consumer, trying to imagine what aspect of the toys would appeal to her. But her thoughts were scattered, interspersed with images of her and Lucas instead of the nameless, faceless lover she usually visualized. She pictured herself chaining Lucas to the big bed in his bedroom, clamping his big wrists with the fuzzy pink cuffs, slipping the blindfold over his eyes, taking away his most powerful sense, and doing naughty things to him while he writhed in pleasure, calling out her name over and over...

"Here you go, Miz Mi." Davy held out a replacement pair of glasses to her. In his other hand he held a plastic shopping bag, probably containing the other eleven or so pairs Crosby wanted.

"Oh, thank you, Davy. These look just like the pair I lost."

"You mean the pair that were stolen, right?" he whispered, his head tucked down, the curtain of his hair partially obscuring his features.

Mi immediately went on alert. Did Davy know

something about their disappearance? "Stolen?" She'd tried for innocence, but sounded suspicious.

"It doesn't take much to figure this is someone's doing. The batteries, the lights, and now your glasses."

"No. I guess not. Do you have any ideas about that, Davy?"

He shook his head, the strands of his long blond hair swishing back and forth. "I'd hate to be him though. Crosby's liable to really lose his temper, and I wouldn't want to be around for that."

Mi cracked a smile, loving Davy all the more for how he took the brunt of Crosby's frustrations with subtle acceptance as if Crosby's angry outbursts couldn't be helped anymore than the sun could stop shining.

"Me either," she said, slipping on the glasses. "But if you hear anything let me know, okay?"

"Sure, sure." He pointed to the products on the table. "I'd better check these over one last time. Don't want you coming across one that doesn't work again."

She resisted the urge to rub his head like a puppy or a small boy. "No, absolutely not. Thank you."

She spotted Lucas at the back of the studio, leaning against the wall, arms crossed, talking with Cal. Even across the distance she could feel his gaze as if he touched her. She had to get a hold of herself, find a way to stop her body from responding to him as though she could be more to him than a job. She was nothing more than a way for him to pay back that favor he owed Cal. She needed to remember that.

"All right, kids. We're a go." Crosby dropped into his director's chair. "Five minutes!"

Tracey rushed over and powdered Mi's face one last time. Davy finished checking the products and arranged them in front of the large centerpiece on the coffee table out of sight from the camera, but within Mi's reach. Other employees scuttled around, performing last minute checks. Then all the lights dimmed in the studio all except those that lit the set. Mi shuffled her note cards back to the beginning. She closed her eyes and mentally gave herself her pre-show pep talk.

"Roll cameras," Crosby barked.

Mi opened her eyes and pasted on her camera smile, the one her viewers trusted.

"Speed," one of the crew answered.

"Begin theme," Crosby directed. "Mi you're on in five, four..." He held up three fingers, then two, then one, and then pointed at Mi to begin.

"Hello and welcome to *Pleasure at Home*. I'm your host, Miyuki. *Pleasure at Home* is America's preferred home shopping show because we bring you products to add spice to your love life or maybe even to help you learn to love yourself a little more. And as always, you can count on *Pleasure at Home* to be discrete with your selections.

"I'm so excited about tonight's show because it's all about couples. Yes, that's right. Our products tonight were chosen with couples in mind to help you get the most pleasure out of your loving relationship..."

At the back of the studio Lucas watched Mi launch

into her spiel. From his vantage point he could see her on the monitors, see what her viewers saw. A confident young woman with an easy smile and soothing voice, Mi oozed trustworthiness and confidentiality. She beckoned her viewers to try something new, to make their fantasies come true and to strengthen their relationships. He could see in a moment why she was so successful.

"This is one of our most profitable shows," Cal whispered. "Couples night is gold." He rubbed his hands together as though preparing them to count stacks of cash.

Mi's voice drifted across the studio. "Our first product of the evening is Mutual Bliss's Thirty-one Flavors Body Paint. Be the canvas as your partner discovers their inner Picasso, painting their way to your mutual gratification…"

Lucas tried not to imagine stroking the paint-dipped brush up and over Mi's hip, down the length of her thigh, and following it with his mouth.

"Completely edible, deliciously decadent, these body paints let you be the artist, designing a night of passion neither one of you will ever forget. Only sixty-three, ninety-nine this delicious palette of pleasure includes such flavors as cherry, chocolate, marshmallow, apple tart, and many more guilt-free taste sensations."

Chocolate tipped nipples… He shuddered, disguising the sudden movement as a simple posture shift. He wondered if anyone would notice if that palette somehow disappeared after the show.

As Mi continued on to the next product, he began to understand the popularity of *Pleasure at Home's* products. He found himself considering the possibilities, as he'd never done before. Maybe it had less to do with his shedding beliefs and more to do with his attraction to Mi. Either way, watching her performance gave him ideas he'd never had before. Not all of the products were for him though. That strap-on thing and that other one for—what the fuck had Mi called it?—'back door action'—were definitely not for him. But those panties with the built-in, controllable vibrator had him smothering a pirate grin.

Cal leaned toward him, pointing at Mi, his lips curved in a cat-that-got-the-cream grin. "Isn't she amazing? And she's all mine. All mine. Remember, I'm counting on you not to let anything happen to my girl."

The way Cal said that with such possession made him wonder for a moment if Cal and Mi had something going. He shot his friend a death stare. Jealousy, hard and sharp stabbed into him, nearly stealing his breath. In a contest between the two of them, Lucas wasn't sure who'd win. The only thing he knew for sure was when it was finally over there'd only be one of them left standing.

And that man had to be Lucas.

5

"I can practically hear my bank balance ticking up and up." Cal's words penetrated Lucas's covetous rage.

As the red haze cleared his vision, Lucas really looked at his friend. Cal had been talking about Mi as though she were a valuable asset, not a lover. A thing to buy, sell or trade. He realized she meant nothing more to Cal than the cameras, the studio or even his precious Mercedes. She was an investment Cal had employed him to protect, nothing more.

He shook his head. What had he been thinking? He'd been thinking with his dick, that's what. Thinking with his dick always gotten him into trouble. Thinking with his dick had allowed Vanessa to fuck him over. And there sat trouble. All one hundred odd pounds of her, holding up a set of fuzzy, pink handcuffs and matching blindfold, looking like every man's fantasy.

Fuck. Fuck. Fuck.

He ran a hand through his hair, knowing he was in

deep. Every time he'd get her within reach she'd slip away. He wondered if it was the chase that enthralled him. He'd never had to chase Vanessa and yet she had never really been his, had she?

Cal mumbled something to him, but his attention remained riveted on Mi. She held up a strange looking rubber ring with a big nub and silver bullet thing attached to it. She switched it on.

"One of our most popular couples toy, the Colossal Cock Ring from Tease and Scream keeps him up and at 'em *all night long*. This powerful couples cock ring delivers a perfect O with a vibrating tongue that hits her spot every time. Only twenty-nine ninety-nine, the variable speed bullet lets you control the intensity wirelessly, so no twisted wires, only tangled limbs and pleasured sighs."

Now that one was on a whole other level. A level he wasn't sure he'd ever be ready for.

"Lucas."

He turned to find Cal regarding him as though he were sizing up a competitor he wanted to take advantage of. Always the worst position to find yourself in with Cal.

"What?"

"I was asking if you and Mi would like to have dinner with me tonight, but I think I already know the answer."

Lucas returned his attention back to Mi, ignoring Cal's bait.

They watched the rest of the show in silence. When it was over, Lucas peeled off the wall with a half-assed muttered goodbye to Cal and followed Mi to the makeup room. Cal's low chuckle followed him.

He stood outside the door, waiting for her to transform back into the fresh-faced Mi he'd come to like best. While he waited, he watched the crew, looking for what he didn't know. A button on a lapel proclaiming allegiance to C.A.L.M.? A receipt for surveillance equipment hanging out a back pocket? Mi's missing glasses clenched in an angry fist? He wished. What he saw was a group of people who worked well together and did their jobs with the practice of long employment.

His phone buzzed in his pocket. He found an out of the way corner from where he could see the doorway to the makeup room and punched the phone on. "Vega."

"The cops are gone." Malcolm said. "They left a right mess."

"I'll take care of it."

"I dropped the key off at your place. The doorman has it."

"Thanks."

"I got news." Malcolm's voice held the excited quiver of a boy who'd pulled the prize from a cereal box.

"Yeah?"

"That background you wanted on Mi?"

With an eye on the doorway, he rolled up to the balls of his feet, his body tensing. "Yeah."

"There's no record of her ever having a child."

He relaxed back down to his heels, but the tension stayed with him. There was more.

"She's never been appointed a legal guardian either."

"Just cut to it," Lucas ground out.

"The only record I could find of a child close to her was a brother born about fourteen years ago. Ethan Derek Easley born July twenty-nine died six months later on January eleven. Cause of death was listed as SIDS, Sudden Infant Death Syndrome."

Lucas thought about the recent photo of Mi and the older woman with a baby in a park. The car seat. The crib. He hadn't bought her explanation about buying those things for Lucy at rummage sales. They'd looked used. And often. Unless she babysat regularly it just didn't add up.

"Anything else?"

"She makes a very decent income, but her bank balance is pathetically low. She has little debt other than her house. No savings. I can't find where her money actually goes. But whatever she's spending it on, she's paying cash, leaving no credit trail." Malcolm let the end of the sentence hang with all kinds of supposition tacked onto it— gambling, drugs, the list went on and on. None of it was good.

Fuck.

"You want me to keep digging?"

That sick feeling he'd gotten, when Vanessa had thrown herself to her knees in front of him begging him to forgive her, dropped into his belly and lay there like a pile of lumber, hard and unrelenting.

"No," he managed. She would have to confide in him on her own.

"Sorry, man."

"Yeah." *Me too,* he silently added. "Thanks. I owe you."

"No. I think giving this kind of news is a favor that should never be repaid." Malcolm hung up.

He shoved his phone deep into his pocket and took a moment to wipe the disappointment from his face. He almost wished he hadn't asked Malcolm to check out Mi. Almost.

He clamped down his emotions, trying not to acknowledge how hard disillusionment rode him. Sifting through the information Malcolm had provided, he compared it with what he'd seen, heard, and surmised about Mi. What was she hiding? And how much of what she was keeping to herself was going to turn around and bite him in the ass?

Mi came out of the makeup room and glanced around until she spotted him. She smiled, her face lit with what looked like genuine pleasure at the sight of him. His forehead hurt and he realized he was scowling back at her. As she neared, he lost all perspective, his vision narrowing down to a point that began and ended with her as though she were a single candle in a darkened room. She came even with him and he realized he'd forgotten to breathe. With his sudden intake of air came the recognition that this tiny woman could do him more harm than a grenade strapped to his chest. It scared him even more that he might be willing to take that risk.

"I'm ready to go." She glanced around the studio. "Is Cal still here?"

"No."

"Oh." She frowned and worried her lip, her gaze darting away. She seemed to be struggling over what to say next. "I... I'm still not quite comfortable with how this works." She made a back and forth motion between them. "I have plans to have dinner with Lucy tonight. I almost forgot until she just texted me." She held out her phone, the screen dark. "I can cancel."

"Up to you."

"Is something wrong?" she asked.

"Hey, Mi," one of the crew guys interrupted. "Crosby wants to see you in his office."

"Thanks, Will."

Lucas trailed after Mi, contemplating calling Cal to ask him to put someone else on Mi. But no. He owed Cal and he'd given his friend his word. Lucas never went back on his word. Never. He'd have to find another way to deal with Mi's deceit. Remembering what he was there to do was a start. Keeping his hands off her and his mind from fantasizing about the things he'd like to do for her... to her... with her... would be near impossible.

They rounded the corner and a man Lucas had never seen before sat in the visitor's chair in Crosby's office. He automatically went for his weapon, stilling when Mi put a hand out to stop him. She recognized the man.

"My brother, Jason."

It took a moment for Lucas to peg the blond-haired kid now grown from the photos at Mi's house. There was no resemblance between them at all.

Where Mi was dark, he was fair. She was petite almost fragile looking, he was tall and broad shouldered. They might be siblings, but they looked nothing alike.

Mi halted in the doorway and cast a quick worried glance back over her shoulder at Lucas before addressing her brother. "What are you doing here?"

"Doing you a damn favor," Jason snapped. "The least you could do is not make me wait. I've got a life, you know."

"Sorry. I didn't know you were here. No one told me."

"Whatever." He waved a hand toward Lucas, his lip curling in a sneer. "Who's big, tall, and grouchy?"

She glanced back and forth between the two men, clearly not wanting to make introductions.

Lucas wasn't going to make things easy on her. He stuck out his hand. "Lucas Vega."

"My boyfriend," Mi finished.

Rising from his chair, Jason ignored Lucas's hand. He stood nearly half a foot shorter than Lucas. But he used his height advantage against Mi, crowding and intimidating her. The punk.

"Boyfriend? Damn it, Mi. *This* is why you called me all desperate for my help? I've got better things to do than babysit a crazy lady so you can screw around with the Hulk here."

Lucas wedged himself between Mi and her brother, putting her behind him, and turned his own height advantage against Jason. "You're going to want to watch how you speak to your sister."

Jason hitched himself up, assessing Lucas and his chances against him. "What are you, her body guard?"

Lucas felt Mi flinch behind him. He took an aggressive, last warning step toward Jason, backing him up a couple of paces.

Jason leaned around Lucas, careful not to touch him. "Call your dog off, Mi or I'm outta here and you're on your own."

Mi gripped Lucas's arm, trying to pull him away from Jason. "Please. It's okay. Let me talk to him."

Lucas spared Jason one last look of reproof, then turned his attention to Mi. "I don't like him."

"Feeling's mutual," Jason muttered behind him.

"He's an ass. But he's your brother." Lucas continued, then turned back to Jason. "You're going to watch how you treat your sister. Got me? I'll be right outside if you need me," he said to Mi as he left.

Mi watched as Lucas shut the door behind him. She put a hand against it to make sure it was fully closed and took a deep, steadying breath before she dealt with her brother.

"What the fuck, Mi? You call me—"

"Keep your voice down," she scolded. He might be bigger than she, but she was the oldest.

"You call me—" he began again in a lower tone. "—to help with mom so you can run around with your new boyfriend. What. The. Fuck. Mi. I have a life, too. A job. You know I hate it when you drag me into mom's shit."

"I didn't drag you into mom's shit—as you put it—for no reason. There's..." Mi didn't know how much she could tell Jason, if anything at all. He was her brother, but the sad fact was he wasn't reliable unless it suited his mood or there was something in it for him. She'd called him out of sheer desperation. He'd agreed reluctantly. His cooperation always came with an expiration date. It looked like time was up.

"You're the worst liar," he accused.

"Why can't you just help me for once? Give me a break. She's your mother, too."

"You know I can't pretend like you do. I hate it, Mi. *Hate* it."

"I'm not asking you to pretend."

He laughed, a smug, know-it-all chuckle that chipped away at Mi's nerves like an ice pick. "I can't believe we're related."

"*Please*, Jas."

His face transformed, turning sharp and calculating. A coldness crept over her and she wondered not for the first time why she continued to protect him. He thought she was an idiot. If he only knew how much he owed her, how she kept the secret that provided him the *life* he so coveted. How much she'd sacrificed for them all.

"Put in a good word for me with that chick you were just talking to," he said.

"Who? Tracey?"

"I don't know her name. Brown hair, big boobs, a mouth that looks like it could suck—"

"Stop!"

"Whatever. You don't need my help *that* bad, I guess."

He made to go around her and out the door, but she put a hand on his arm, stopping him. She looked up into the same winter-blue sky eyes their mother had and couldn't stop the bending of her heart. He was her brother. The only brother she had left. She'd do anything for him. Too bad the feeling wasn't mutual.

"Tracey's my friend."

He crossed his arms over his chest and she noticed he'd been working out, bulking up. Not that he ever needed help with the ladies. He was way too handsome for his own good. Women swarmed like flies to horse manure, which she was sure he was shoveling her direction now.

"Since when do you need help talking to a woman?" she asked.

"I don't."

"So what gives?"

"If you don't want my help, I'll just go talk to her myself."

Now she got it. It wasn't about his needing an introduction, it was about who was in control. Him. It was her fault he was the way he was. She'd done the best she could raising him, but her best wasn't even close to good enough. He'd grown up in a household out of control. She could hardly blame him now for trying to claim a little control where he could. Even if it cost her.

"Fine," she agreed on a sigh.

"Yes. I. *Certainly*. Am. Mom says hi, by the way. She wanted to come with me, but it was *Ethan's* nap time." His lips pressed into an unattractive line. "Did I mention the part where I. Hate. Pretending? *Hate* it."

Mi eased into a chair and closed her eyes, rubbing at her temples. She hated it, too. The pretending. But as long as mom was stable. What choice was there?

"I know." She pulled in a breath and exhaled hard, showing him how exhausted this made her. She was so tired of it all. The tightrope walk between the secret that kept their mother sane and the one that kept them all out of jail. Thirteen years was a long time to hold it all together.

"I don't know why you do it, Mi." He looked down at her, a lock of blond hair falling over one eye, and she saw the boy he'd been. The lonely boy who had no friends because his mother embarrassed him. The fearful boy who spent all his time alone in his room rather than face what awaited him if he crossed his mother. The angry boy who got thought of last because he didn't need as much attention as their mother demanded.

She stood up and wrapped her arms around her brother, thinking- *No, you don't. You don't have any idea what I've done for you. What I continue to do. I'd do for anything for you. You and mom are all I have.*

He took a half step back in surprise and then he slowly enveloped her in a hug that was tentative at best. At worst it was awkward and unwanted. He released her almost as soon as he'd started and moved to the door.

"Come on, Sis. Introduce me to Tracey of tremendous ta-tas," he threw out over his shoulder as he stepped into the hall.

They each had their own defense mechanisms she

guessed. His was a crude attempt a humor, playing his role as the worthless younger brother to the hilt. Hers was avoidance, dealing only with what was in front of her and then only if she had to. She wondered what they'd be to each other if one of them suddenly decided not to play their part anymore. Would they like each other or continue to barely tolerate one another? Would they even recognize each other? Would they recognize themselves?

Who was Jason if he wasn't constantly disappointing her? Who was she if she wasn't constantly disappointing him? Who were they as a family without the blame, resentment and anger?

MI MET Lucy at a local Tex-Mex restaurant that boasted thirty kinds of *quesadillas* and chocolate caramel *nachos* that was Lucy's craving of the week. Mi tried not to think about Jason or her mom, but it was always there, throbbing and flaring into new pain like a chronic toothache. Lucas had been silent on the drive over. Mi wasn't sure what that was about. Maybe he was tired of following her around. She wondered about his life. He'd pretty much given up his for hers. From what he'd told her he seemed to be at a crossroads, deciding what to do for employment. She didn't think he had a girlfriend, at least she hoped not after the kisses they'd shared.

Thinking about those kisses, she tried not to shift in her seat. Heat shimmered within her, like the waves still dancing over the pavement even though it was nearly dusk now. She pretended to look over the menu while she waited for Lucy to show, watching Lucas through lowered lashes. He'd situated himself at a nearby table with his back to the wall and a clear view of the room. The sight of him did funny things to her. That low hum pulsed almost constantly, taking up residence in places long neglected.

Not smart, she reminded herself. Their differences stacked up higher than the Dallas skyline. He'd been clear about his views on what she did for a living. Jason's visit had reminded her of all the reasons she hadn't gotten involved with anyone seriously in a long time. Then there were the differences in their lifestyles. Images of his home superimposed over images of hers, bringing the depressing reality that they came from very different backgrounds. And to top it off he hated her brother. Well, she couldn't really blame him for that one.

Lucy walked through the door, bringing a radiance with her that lit the entire room. Just the sight of her brought Mi so much joy, her face split into a grin she couldn't control. Flushed from the lingering heat and glow of pregnancy, Lucy looked stunning in a yellow and white gingham halter dress trimmed in white eyelet. She'd pulled her long blond hair back into a ponytail that trailed nearly to her waist. When she spotted Mi her face broke into a wide smile and she waved. Heads turned to follow her movement across the restaurant, regardless of her hugely swollen belly, as she picked her way toward Mi.

Lucy hugged her with the exuberance of a long lost relative. "Oh, I missed you," she gushed, her east Texas accent slow and melodic. "How are you?"

"I'm good. Look at you!" Mi couldn't get over how much her friend's body had changed in the couple of weeks since she'd seen her. "Your boobs are huge," she blurted out without meaning to.

"I know. Kevin can't get enough of them." She giggled, her laugh infectious, inviting Mi and everyone else to join in the merriment. "I hardly fit into anything anymore. I'm so huge." She didn't seem unhappy about it instead she seemed thrilled as though nothing better could have happened to her.

They slid into the booth and scooted in next to each other. It felt so good to be with Lucy, like lying in the sun on a tropical beach.

"How are you feeling?" Mi asked.

"Gigantic, but the doctor says everything's right on schedule. Which is good because Kevin planned his business trip around my due date. He doesn't want to be in Cincinnati or Denver when little Jessalyn arrives." She patted her belly, beaming a smile that showed signs of overuse.

"He's been out of town a lot lately."

"His consulting business has really taken off." Lucy grabbed a chip from the basket the waiter had brought, broke it in half and dunked it in salsa. "Which is good because we could really use the money for all of the things little Brie needs." She popped the chip in her mouth with a frown slightly creasing her brow.

"Wait. Which is it, Brie or Jessalyn?"

"Oh, I can't decide! I change my mind every other day. Kevin likes Jessalyn, but I don't know." She scrunched up her cute little nose. "Sounds old fashioned to me. We both like the name Brie though."

"But you always told me that if you have a girl you'd name her Poppy after your grandma."

"Kevin doesn't like the name Poppy. He says it's a silly name." Her perpetual grin slipped a little before she caught it and propped it back up.

"Is everything all right between you two?"

"Kevin and me?" Lucy glanced off to the side, concentrating on dipping another chip. "Why sure, sweetie. Couldn't be better."

Mi didn't believe her. Something was off. "And everything's okay with the baby?"

Her smile returned tenfold. "Oh, yes. She's going to be so perfect. I can't wait. I set up the nursery with all of the things I got from my shower. It's so pretty. You have to come and see. Kevin still has to put the crib together, but he says there will be plenty of time for that when he gets back."

Their waiter arrived and took their order. As soon as he left, Lucy put a hand over her mouth and whispered. "See that man over there by the potted fern? He's been staring this direction. I know he's not looking at me with my big, giant belly." She nudged Mi. "He's a big one and kind of handsome in a scary bad-boy sort of way. Oh! He looked over again. He's definitely looking at you."

"That's Lucas."

"You know him?"

Mi sighed. "He's my bodyguard." She dove into the story about why she needed Lucas. When she finished, Lucy was looking at her with a mixture of horror and shock.

"Oh, sweetie. You poor thing. Well, that just isn't right." Lucy slapped a hand on the table, making their silverware dance. "I can't believe Cal could be so cheap as to get you a bodyguard for free! Calling in a favor." She shook her head, her ponytail swaying with her irritation. "That cheap son of a bitch makes more money than God and that computer guy put together. He can afford a whole team of bodyguards. Not that big, tall, and brooding over there couldn't handle himself real good in a fight or anything. I just think you deserve better."

"I don't know what I'd do with a whole army of men following me around all day." The thought of that alternative gave Mi a bad moment. "I'm fine with Lucas. Cal's increasing security at the studio both inside and out. The police are on top of the case. The detective in charge told me it's just a matter of time before they catch up to Doyle Gann and when they do, they'll likely revoke his parole. In the meantime, I feel perfectly safe with Lucas."

Lucy eyed Lucas's profile, then looked at Mi, then to Lucas and back again. "I think that tall, dark drink of water wants to do more to your body than protect it." She nodded as if confirming her own thoughts. "A lot more."

Mi's cheeks flamed and she ducked her head, sure

Lucas overheard Lucy's comment even though he showed no reaction.

"Sweetie," Lucy said, her Texas drawl slower than molasses over ice. "I know when a man's interested. Believe me. And that man is interested with a capitol I-want-you-naked."

"Lucy," Mi begged.

Their server appeared with their order. "Is there anything else I can get you?" he asked.

"No, darlin'. We're fine," Lucy answered.

"Okay, just let me know." The server started to leave, then turned back and pulled an envelope from his apron pocket. He handed it to Mi. "I was told to give this to you"

Mi accepted the envelope automatically. "Who is it from?"

He hitched a shoulder already moving on to another table. "Don't know. He gave me twenty bucks to give it to you with your food."

Mi stared down at the envelope, then back up at the server, but he was already gone.

"I don't think it's from a secret admirer," Lucy said, eyeing the envelope as though it were a coiled rattlesnake.

Mi looked at Lucy and the envelope was snatched out of her hands.

"You're not opening this." Lucas towered over her, looking prepared to do damage. He held up a hand. "Stay here."

They watched as Lucas stormed over to the server, grabbed him by the back of the shirt and marched him back to their table. He held the guy up so that his feet barely touched the floor. He thrust the envelope in the guy's face. "Who gave this to you?"

"I don't know, man."

"What did he look like?"

"I don't know! A guy. A white guy."

"Is he still here?" Lucas asked, scanning the restaurant.

"No, man. He gave me the envelope and a twenty, then split."

The waiter looked like he'd piss himself, but Lucas didn't care. He gave the kid a shake. "Dark hair? Light hair? Old? Young?"

"Don't hit me," the guy whined, putting his hands up in front of his face.

"Lucas." Mi gripped the wrist of the hand he was holding the letter in. "Lucas, please stop. You're scaring him."

He looked down at Mi's wide eyes and then over at the punk dangling from his fist. He hooked a chair with his foot and dropped the guy down onto it gentler than he would have if Mi hadn't been staring at him with her golden eyes full of fear. Of him.

Fuck.

"I take it back, sweetie," Lucy said to Mi from behind her hand. "That son of a bitch, Cal, did right by you after all."

Ignoring Lucy's comment, Lucas pulled a chair up even with the kid and sat across from him. "I need to know everything you can remember about the guy who gave you this envelope. What he looked like, what he said, how he acted, everything."

A man with a name badge declaring him 'manager' appeared. "Is everything all right here?"

Mi scooted to the edge of the booth, swung her legs over the edge and stood up. "Yes, thank you everything's fine. Billy here, gave me an envelope from a secret admirer and my boyfriend—" She motioned toward Lucas. "—got a little jealous. He wants to know who his competition is. Not that he has any." Mi flashed Lucas a smile that made it clear he had no rival. "Sorry for the commotion."

"He's got tables waiting," the manager informed them before walking away with a warning glare.

When the manager was out of earshot, Mi put a hand on Billy's shoulder and leaned in. "I'm sorry to cause you trouble, but we need your help. Can you tell me about the man who gave you the envelope?"

Billy cast Lucas a wary glance and straightened in his chair. "Sure." His voice came out unsteady. He cleared his throat. "He had black hair with some gray."

"Okay, that's good. What else?" Mi asked.

"Dark eyes. Kind of small and close together. He was a little taller than me so maybe five-ten, five-eleven?"

Mi nodded in encouragement.

"And a scar. Right here." Billy drew a line on his face over his left eye from hairline to eyebrow.

"Is this the guy?" Lucas asked, holding up his cell phone for Billy to see.

Billy bobbed his head. "That looks like him, but he didn't have a beard."

"Who is it?" Mi tried to peer around to see the phone screen.

Lucas turned the phone so only he could see it and looked at the face of a convicted murderer.

Doyle Gann.

6

Lucas dropped a hundred dollar bill on the table. "Thank you for your help. The police are going to want to talk to you about what you saw."

Billy put up his hands. "No, man. No police."

Lucas peeled off another hundred. "What's your full name and cell number?"

The kid had the nerve to eye the bundle in Lucas's hand a little too covetously.

"Don't push your luck and I won't tell your manager that you're undercharging the customers and pocketing the difference."

The kid rattled off his info as Lucas punched it into his phone.

"Let's go," he said to Mi. "Nice meeting you, Lucy."

"Likewise, I'm sure." Lucy hugged Mi and he could hear her whisper as if she were speaking in his own ear instead of Mi's. "You need a take-charge man like *him* in your life, sweetie. Think about it."

As Lucas and Mi set off toward the exit, a cell phone rang behind them. Lucas turned back to the kid. "Just checking. Take my calls. Don't make me find you."

He tucked Mi into his side with an arm around her as they made their way through the restaurant. He grunted in satisfaction at the feel of Mi fisting the back of his shirt in her small hand, holding on tight as he propelled them toward the exit.

Putting Mi a little behind him, Lucas scanned the now darkened street. Sunset had cooled the air, but the pavement retained the heat of the day like hearthstones after a fire. A flimsy breeze greeted them as they stepped out onto the sidewalk, joining the other pedestrians out for a night stroll. Senses on high alert, Lucas moved quickly. He hoisted Mi up, basically carrying her at his side on the short walk to his truck. He clicked the car locks off and lifted Mi in and over the center console. He didn't register the flash of pink lace her hiked up skirt had exposed until they were several blocks away.

"It was Doyle Gann, wasn't it?" Mi asked a short time later, her voice calm.

She'd held it together, going along with him without asking questions. But now he could see the strain in the brief glimpses he caught of her face in the strobe effect of the streetlights.

He wasn't going to hide the facts from her. She needed to know what she was up against. He knew she could handle it. "Yes."

She didn't speak for a few moments so he checked

on her. She was working that lip again, but her head was up, her shoulders back.

She angled her body toward his. "What do you think is in the envelope?"

"Does it matter?"

"No, I suppose not."

"He's not going to get to you, Mi."

"How can you be so sure?"

"Because he'd have to go through me."

She nodded as if accepting his boast as fact. Satisfaction swelled within him. She trusted him. He reached across the console and took her hand in his. A comfortable silence drifted over them like a blanket, each of them immersed in their own thoughts.

Checking his mirrors frequently, Lucas took a round about way back to his apartment. He drove past the parking garage twice from two different directions before clicking the door open and rolling the truck into his assigned parking space.

Mi turned her body toward him, her focus on their joined hands. "Lucy was right. Cal did pick the right man to protect me. Thank you."

He could just make out her features in the dim yellow light of the underground garage. She looked so earnest in her gratitude that it pricked his temper. He didn't want her gratitude. He wanted her, panting and writhing beneath him, screaming his name. She could thank him for that.

He reached for her none too gently, pulling her as close as the console allowed. She let him, tipping her head back to look up at him. He froze, lost in the look in her eyes. She wanted him. The knowledge stunned him. Lowering his mouth to hers, he maintained eye contact, allowing her that small chance to back out. She met him half way, reaching to bring him closer. And then they were kissing. He fought to keep it light. Fought hard.

She sighed into the kiss, threading her fingers into his hair, and the fight became a battle. He wanted to crush her to him, devour her. She climbed over the console into his lap, straddling him. Gripping her ass, he pulled her down against his erection. She wiggled, grinding into him, and he nearly lost it. Nearly ripped at her clothes to get inside her. He slipped a hand under her skirt, up her bare thigh, and pressed his thumb to her. Jesus, she was wet. For him. He could smell her, hot and ready. He reached for her panties with both hands. Allowing him, she arched back and leaned into the horn. Startled, Mi jumped and accidentally hit the horn again.

She collapsed against his chest, laughing. "I feel like a teenager about to get busted."

His heart thundered like the boom of a howitzer, half lust and half scared shitless. He was a fucking idiot. They were totally exposed. He had to get Mi out of here and into the safety of the apartment.

Wrapping his arms around her, he brought her close, marveling at the feel of her body against his. God, she was so small, so perfect. He breathed in her perfume mixed with the scent of her arousal. Jesus. He needed her upstairs safe... and naked. Now.

With regret he untangled her fingers from his hair

and kissed her palms, one then the other. "We need to get you inside," he murmured in her ear. She shivered. Jesus.

It took everything in him to lift her off of him and onto the center console. He needed both of his hands. Pulling his gun from his waistband, he put up a hand for her to stay put. She nodded, hugging herself. He opened the car door and climbed out, scanning the garage for movement. He knew no one had followed them in. Assured they were alone in the garage, he motioned for her to climb out of the truck and had to give her a hand down.

They hustled into the building, his senses amped. As they reached the lobby, he tucked his gun away. They rode up to his apartment in silence. Mi seemed absorbed in the changing floor numbers. She had some red marks on her neck and chest, razor burn. He liked his mark on her. Her hair was messy and a couple buttons on her shirt had popped open to reveal a pink bra that matched her panties. She looked tumbled. He'd have given anything right then to find out what she looked like completely satisfied... by him.

The doors whooshed open to the entryway of his apartment. Taking her hand, he backed into the apartment, pulling her along with him. He couldn't take his eyes off her. She was amazing, sexy as hell, and he wanted her with a hunger that nearly snapped his control. She leaned back and let him drag her off the elevator with a shy smile. Thank God she was smiling and not running from the wolfish grin he hoped promised her pleasure.

She came to a stuttering stop just over the threshold. Her look of surprise made him spin. He shoved her quickly behind him.

He couldn't fucking believe it. "What the hell are you doing here, Vanessa?"

His ex-fiancée stood in the middle of his living room with a box propped on her hip. She'd let her auburn hair grow nearly to her waist. Her breasts strained against the fabric of her wrap dress. Everything about her was fuller, lusher than he remembered. And she didn't do a damn thing for him. Huh.

"I came to return some things I had of yours." She offered up the box. "And to... talk." She pushed out her lower lip and tilted her head in that way that normally would have had him panting at her side.

"There's nothing to talk about." He folded his arms over his chest.

Mi stepped out from behind him. "I think I'll just go to my room."

"Stay." He gave Vanessa a hard look from head to toe, looking for what he didn't know. Realization hit with the shock of diving into an ice-cold ocean. He felt nothing for her. The immense power she'd had over him was gone, leaving behind nothing but a thin film of disgust. "*She's* leaving."

"Who are you?" Vanessa asked, running her gaze up and down Mi, clearly finding nothing but fault with what she saw. She'd always been a fucking snob.

"Get out," Lucas repeated.

Vanessa set the box down on the hideous couch she'd picked out along with all the other crap in the apartment that she'd called cutting edge. "I'm Vanessa," she said, crossing an arm across her body and propping her elbow in her hand. The pose did great things for her breasts, pushing them up and out. "Lucas's fiancée." Her finger rested just below her lower lip, purposefully drawing the eye there while giving her an air of superiority and showing off the engagement ring he'd given her. "And you are...?"

"None of your goddamned business," he roared out of a combination of a fading hard on and ex-bitch-fiancée annoyance. "And you forgot the ex part of fiancée. I don't know what you think you're doing here—"

"Oh, Lucas." She actually had the fucking nerve to look hurt.

Mi made a move past him. He reached for her, but she slipped away from him. The bedroom door closed behind her with a click that echoed in his brain like a gunshot.

He turned on Vanessa, his temper dangerously close to exploding. "Get the fuck out. Now."

"Please listen. I made a mistake." She sidled up next to him. Her smell curled around him, nauseating him. "I know that now." She ran a finger down his neck, flattening her hand against his chest as she stroked her way down. "I miss you," she whispered.

Nothing. Not a damn thing. She'd used her best tricks. And they did nothing for him. He lifted her hand off of him by the wrist. Keeping hold of her, he reached around and grabbed the box she'd brought. He pushed it at her and punched the elevator button. "You're leaving and you're never coming back. Give me your key."

Shock, then anger flashed across her pretty face. "You can't mean that."

He gave her a get-real glare and held out his hand. "The key, Vanessa."

"Please, Lucas. I'm sorry. I love you, baby. I made a mistake. I know that now. Please forgive me and I'll forget all about *her*." She tilted her head in the direction Mi had gone. "We were good together, remember?"

Oh, he remembered.

"Last chance," he warned.

She'd worked up a tear and it slid down her cheek, catching at the corner of her mouth. Another tear fell, landing on the back of his hand still holding her wrist. She was a master at sorry. Too bad she hadn't bothered to learn faithful and honest.

"I don't want you, Vanessa. Now or ever. All I want from you is my key and for you to leave. And not come back."

Her eyes widened, then narrowed. She reached into her purse and pulled out the key card to his apartment. Waving in front of his face, she finally came around to the real reason for her visit. "How much will you give me for it?"

To her surprise, he snatched it cleanly. The elevator door whooshed open behind him. "Goodbye, Vanessa." He moved her toward the open doors.

Always needing the final word, she played her last trick. Dropping the box at his feet, she twisted free from his grip. "You always were a cold son of a bitch. Is it any wonder I sought heat elsewhere?" She flicked a wrist toward the bedroom where Mi had escaped. "She will too. You're a shark, cold and flat, taking bites out of people until there's nothing left. The only reason I stayed as long as I did was your money." She stepped into the elevator and jabbed a button. "But in the end, even that wasn't enough." The doors closed on her parting shot.

He stood there frozen, meeting his own gaze in the dull reflection of the doors. Cold. He'd heard that before. *You don't feel the way other people do*, his mother had told him. *Just like your grandfather*. The man he'd been named after, the coldest son of a bitch who'd ever walked the earth. His ruthless business practices were legendary. Even now—three years after his death—the name Joaquin Lucas Vega struck fear in the business world. His brutal practice of stripping companies to their most profitable denominator had made him a millionaire many times over. He'd not thought twice about the destroyed lives he'd left in his wake.

Lucas had inherited that coldness. He saw it in the way people reacted to him, giving him a wide berth, avoiding eye contact. Hell, Mi had been afraid of him when they'd met, flinching at his nearness. There'd been times since when he'd caught her watching him as though he were an off-leash junkyard dog. He'd seen her uncertainty, wanting to touch him, and yet half afraid she'd pull back a bloody stump.

He slammed the palm of his hand into his reflection, leaving a dent in the panel. Shaking out his hand, he turned away from those thoughts and the damage he'd done. Mi stood in the opening of the living room, the dark hall stretched out behind her. Her face reflected the turmoil inside him. She'd taken a reflexive step backward. Her body balanced between going back the way she'd come and moving into the room with him.

He faced her across the span of the room, feeling the new distance between them like a yawning gap with no bridge. He held down the panic and self-loathing and focused on her.

"Are you hungry? You never got to eat your dinner with Lucy."

"I'm okay."

He remained where he was, waiting for her to decide about him. "I'm sorry about Vanessa. I forgot she still had a key." Even to his ears that sounded lame. "She's gone." *State the fucking obvious.* "Sure you're not hungry? I am. My dinner hadn't arrived when we left. We could order in."

She took a couple of steps forward, but he didn't dare twitch even a finger. "Actually, yes. I am. What are the options?"

"I have some take-out menus in a drawer in the kitchen." He risked lifting a hand toward the kitchen. "I'll get them and you can decide." He waited for her nod to move slowly in the direction of the kitchen. "Would you like a drink?" he called over his shoulder as he reached the entry of the kitchen.

"Whatever you're having," she answered.

He rifled through the drawer, finding a fistful of menus. When he turned, she stood in the doorway, watching him with a wariness that made the space between his shoulder blades itch.

"There's Italian. Chinese. Mexican." She shook her head at the last suggestion, her face scrunching into a smile that was all eyes and no teeth.

He tried a laugh. "No, I guess not. There's a deli around the corner that delivers."

"That sounds good." She held out her hand. "Can I see the menu?"

THEY ATE their submarine sandwiches and potato salad at the dining room table. The jagged metal and glass chandelier hung over them like a flail mid swing. Mi flicked uncertain glances between it and Lucas, trying to decide which was the prickliest. Clearly Vanessa's unexpected visit had shaken him. She wondered if he still had feelings for Vanessa. From his reaction she didn't think so. But Vanessa had hurt him that much was clear. Mi was sure that whatever had happened between the two of them was Vanessa's doing, not Lucas's.

Poor Lucas. He'd been embarrassed that she'd witnessed his loss of control. She hadn't been sure how to approach him afterward so she took her cue from him by pretending he hadn't put a fist sized dent in his elevator door.

She was beginning to learn that Lucas often shut down or became angry in defense against emotion. Almost as though he could put his emotions into neat little compartments to deal with later... or not. That skill must have been an asset to him in the military. She looked up through her lashes at him, watching him systematically devour his dinner with the precision of an infantry drill.

"How's your food?" he asked.

"Very good." She looked down at the wrapper in front of her with nothing left on it but a blob of mayonnaise and a few shreds of lettuce. "I didn't realize how hungry I was."

"I called Detective Rolls about the incident at the restaurant."

She nodded. The feeling of being hunted came back to her ten-fold. She clamped down on it, shoving it down deep with all of the other emotions she couldn't allow. She wished she had Lucas's skill in handling her emotions. Hers weren't neat. They were a jumbled, tangled mess that bubbled and spat at the lid she tried to keep over them.

He wiped his mouth with a napkin, got up, and cleared the table. She watched his controlled movements in fascination. His restraint was incredible. She only pretended at control, just barely managing to keep it together. Knowing at any moment she could lose the battle and end up like her mother.

"Would you like a beer?" he asked.

"Only if you'll have one with me," she half joked.

He paused, looking down at her, his lips pressed into a deep frown. "I would. But after what happened today..." Something close to regret dug a furrow between his brows and he placed a hand on her cheek, stroking the pad of his thumb across her cheekbone. "I won't take any chances with you."

She nodded, tilting her head into his caress. "I understand." And she did. Whatever she was to him now was more than just a job. The thrumming he caused deep within her shimmered and shook, quivering so keenly she could hardly contain it. She closed her eyes, savoring the sensation.

He kneeled down in front of her. "Mi."

Her lashes fluttered open and she found herself staring into eyes the color of a night sea, dark and fathomless. He leaned forward slowly, always slowly. *Too* slowly. She placed her hands on either side of his face and hurried him along. The first brush of his lips had her turning in her chair, scooting toward him. He wound his arms around her, bringing her flush against him, and changed the angle of the kiss, still keeping it light. His body was hot and hard in all the right places. She inhaled his scent like drug. It got inside her and she knew for as long as she lived she'd associate the smell of him with warm nights and a yearning so fierce she wanted to rip her clothes off and present herself for his pleasure.

He moaned, a sound both plaintive and aching as he pulled away from her. "Detective Rolls is sending someone over for the envelope." He set his forehead to hers. "He should be here any moment."

"Okay." He stood to leave, but she grabbed his wrist, stopping him. "I just wanted to say thank you. For dinner. For letting me stay here. And for being so good at your job." She pulled on his wrist for emphasis. "Thank you. For everything."

He looked away, his jaw working, then turned back angry. "You can thank me by not thanking me."

"I just... I'm sorry."

Bracketing her with a hand on her chair and a hand on the table, he leaned down. "I don't want your apologies either," he said, his voice rough and agitated.

"Wh... what do you want?"

The doorbell rang. He didn't look away at the sound or start as she did.

"You." And then he was gone in a fleeting movement that left behind nothing, but the echo of his hard footsteps on the tile floor.

She sat for a moment, dazed. Her hand fluttered to her throat where her pulse jumped in time with her heart and pounded in her ears. She couldn't catch her breath. The room seemed to disappear. Her senses extinguished, leaving her with nothing, but the simple knowledge that Lucas wanted her. He'd had Vanessa. He'd probably had many beautiful women, but now he wanted her. Tiny, freckled, freakish her.

She didn't dare to hope. Didn't dare to dream. He was attracted to her, she knew. Past that she hadn't seen. Hadn't thought to look. And why would she?

"Meow." Gooch sat at her feet, staring up at her with his giant marble eyes.

She bent and picked him up, nuzzling him to her. "Well, hello, Mr. Gooch. Where have you been hiding?"

Voices intruded on her thoughts from the other room, both male. She should probably go in there and give her accounting of what happened at the restaurant.

The cat wiggled in her hands so she put him down on the table in front of her.

"He's a complicated man," she told the cat. He stared back at her. "I have a complicated life. This could... complicate things... even more." He blinked. "Then again—"

Gooch yawned and curled up on the placemat, winding his tail around to his nose.

"Well." She exhaled hard. "He doesn't strike me as the kind of man who would say something like that just to get into my pants. He wouldn't have to. He's been nearly there just about every time he's touched me." She frowned over that. "Maybe I've made it too easy for him. What do you think?" Silence. "Don't judge me. He's seriously hot. And when he touches me, well... wow. Big wow. Fireworks and lightening wow."

Gooch's brows twitched.

"He wants me." She hugged Lucas's declaration to her a moment more, then with a long sigh she put away her hope, picked up the cat and went into the other room.

7

For the next few days Lucas gave Mi some space, keeping his hands mostly to himself. He'd been clear about what he wanted. Now it was up to her.

The wait was killing him.

She'd received a phone call yesterday morning that she'd rushed to the privacy of her bedroom to take. When she'd emerged, she'd been trembling and had a hard time meeting his gaze. Since then she'd avoided his touch, but a few times he'd caught her watching him with a look that nearly scorched his skin. She wanted him. So who or what was holding her back?

He thought about calling Malcolm back to dig deeper into her background or at the very least get a copy of her phone records to find out who she'd spoken to. But honor got the better of him and he couldn't do it. As her bodyguard he'd be entitled to find out as much as he could about her and her life by whatever means necessary. As her lover—damn, just the thought—he expected total honesty. Anything less was unacceptable. And this he suddenly realized was the possible reason she held back.

So he'd wait. With the worst case of blue balls since his high school days when he'd dated Wendy I'm-saving-myself-for-marriage Conrad. *Those* were six of the longest months of his life. He hadn't been half as attracted to Wendy as he was to Mi. Living with Mi and not having her was liable to kill him. Hopefully it would be a quick death.

It was Friday and Mi had just finished taping her last show of the week. They'd been told to wait in Crosby's office with no further explanation. Lucas hung out in the hall near the door, unable to stand being in the same confining space with Mi and not be able to touch her.

She sat at the edge of her chair, jiggling her leg, and biting her lip. He overrode his instinct to go to her and hold her or distract her with a kiss. Instead he paced the short hall, like a caged panther, feeling more than a little restless and edgy. He needed a good long run or a hard workout in the gym. Vigorous hand-to-hand combat that left him sweaty and exhausted would work just as well. No, better. Bodies entwined, grappling for purchase...

Fuck.

"Where's Mi?" Crosby growled from behind him.

Lucas gestured toward the doorway.

"Get in there. I need to talk to the both of you."

Lucas shuffled in behind Crosby and closed the door. He stood rather than sat next to Mi.

Crosby opened a desk drawer and rummaged around. He grunted when he'd finally found what he'd been looking for—a silver flask. He took a long pull, capped it, and dropped it back in the drawer, shoving it closed with his foot.

Leaning back in his chair, Crosby divided his blood shot gaze between the two of them as he spoke. "I'm told C.A.L.M. has Senator Vasquez and Congress... person—" He rolled his eyes. "—Williams on board with their goddamned agenda. Which means someone gave a helluva lot of money to their campaigns.

"It also means that more idiots are going to pay that goddamned Stepford bitch-wife Cookie Dixon and her crazies even more attention. We're going to have the goddamned media crawling up our asses, trying to get quotes. Don't do it. Not one goddamned word. You hear me?"

He pointed a finger at each one of them in turn, eliciting their agreement. When they'd both nodded yes, Crosby continued in a gentler tone for Mi. "How're you holding up, Kid?"

"I'm okay."

"I hear you had a scare."

"It wasn't so bad."

Crosby gave her a disbelieving glare. "Don't placate me like some goddamned grandfather! I know more about this goddamned shit than you do, so don't bull-shit me. You hear?"

"Yes, Crosby."

"And you." He turned his attention to Lucas, making him straighten up from the wall. "You're glue.

You stick to her like goddamned white on rice. *You* hear?"

"Yes, sir."

"And remember that other thing I told you. I'm not too old to kick your ass from here to Albuquerque. And I'll do it, too. Just try me."

"Crosby," Mi begged.

Lucas actually broke out in a sweat as if he was standing on his girlfriend's porch with his hands on her tits, staring down the barrel of her father's sawed-off shotgun. "Yes, sir. I remember."

Mi buried her face in her hands, red-hot embarrassment flooding her from head to toe. She loved Crosby and knew he loved her, but sometimes being treated like one his daughters was... difficult.

Crosby subsided with a firm nod. "That's all. Get out of here. And take care of my girl!" he added as they hit the hall.

Lucas dropped behind her as they made their way through the building to the exit. He'd pulled back from her since the night he told her he wanted her, limiting his touches to only those that were necessary. She more than missed the feel of his hands on her. She ached for him.

She'd nearly gone to him last night, needing his strength and ever-present promise of pleasure. Her mother, Faye Easley, had called her that morning, sounding more fractured than she had since the months after Ethan's birth. She'd begged Mi to come and see her. Her nonsensical ramblings about visions and dreams, reminded Mi of those days thirteen years ago when Faye's unpredictable behavior brought nights of sheer terror.

The nights had been the worst.

Faye's dreams spilled over into waking nightmares for Mi and her brother Jason. On several occasions Mi had woken up to find their mother roaming the halls, mumbling frightening things about demons and murder. Once Mi found her leaning over Ethan's crib with a pillow in her hand. After that, Mi had slept in the hall outside Ethan's room. Sitting with her back pressed to the wall, Mi had forced herself to stay awake night after night.

Terrorized by their mother's behavior, ten year-old Jason went into a tailspin, acting out in school and sleepwalking. With Mi's father dead since she was two, Jason's father gone for more years than he'd stayed, and little Ethan's father a mystery, Jason had turned to Mi for the things a parent should have done. She took on the role, doing the best her fifteen year-old self could to hold her family together.

Mi became the keeper of secrets and the protector of her family.

Until the night she failed.

And now it seemed she might fail them again. Sniffing back sudden tears, Mi ducked into the ladies room only to find Lucas had followed her in.

"Can't I ever be alone?" she barked at him.

He ignored her, opening one stall door then another. When he'd cleared them all, he walked out without a word. She knew he'd be waiting outside the door.

She wanted to hit something, preferably him. Instead she ran the tap and splashed cold water on her face and neck. The chill water soothed the ache behind her eyes, but did little to relieve the frustration riding her.

When she came out of the bathroom, he was there, waiting. She motioned for him to proceed. In silence they performed the ritual of exiting the building, like a well-choreographed dance. He swept the area, gun drawn, and walked around the truck, peering inside and under. When he was satisfied, he returned for her, bundled her into the truck, and then they were on their way. To *his* apartment.

Nothing was hers anymore. Not the car she rode in, the house where she lived, the decisions she made, how she spent her time. She couldn't even go to the bathroom without the production of a full room sweep.

And she hated it.

Guilt burned a hole in her stomach. She should be grateful, not resentful. He was there to keep her safe, but after a week of being guarded twenty-four seven she was damn sick of what her life had become.

Lucas drove around the building toward the gate and her attitude instantly changed. Her annoyance melted into relief, her resentment became gratitude as she sank into the foot well of the truck out of sight of the crowd, which had doubled again in size thanks to the news vans clogging the street.

Lucas muttered an expletive, his dark gaze narrowed. "Keep down. This crowd's out for blood."

She made herself as small as possible, wedging

between the dash and floor. Their getaway was quicker than usual thanks to Cal's added security, which had cleared a lane wide enough for them to pass. The shouts and jeers—although muffled in the truck's interior—crashed around her, like brutal waves in an ocean of hate. She clapped her hands over her ears and squeezed her eyes shut.

After a few minutes, she felt a hand on her arm and opened her eyes to find Lucas looking down at her. "It's all right. You can sit up now. We're well past them."

She climbed up into her seat and clicked on her seat belt.

"Now I Lay Me Down to Sleep?" he asked.

"What?"

"That's what you kept saying over and over."

"Oh. I was trying to drown out the voices."

The corners of his mouth kicked up into a rare smile. "It was cute."

"I guess it's better than la-la-la-la-la."

Stopped at a light, he gave her a slow appraisal, the smile warming his eyes to melting dark chocolate. "You're holding up well. I'm impressed. I've seen battle-hardened sailors who've caved under less stress."

She wasn't holding up, she was barely holding on. Not sure how to answer, she didn't.

"Are you hungry?" he asked.

She wondered if he realized what a caretaker he was, often asking how she was, if she wanted anything. And he always made sure she ate. It was a strange feeling being on the receiving end. She didn't dare get used to it.

"You know what sounds good?" she replied. "Pizza. My treat."

His hesitation and deep frown told her he wasn't comfortable with her paying for anything, but he gave in. "Sounds good. But no pineapple."

She mock shuddered. "Absolutely not. You want pineapple, you pay."

They rode back to his apartment in silence, but it was an easy kind of quiet, like that shared by friends or lovers. She was grateful for the peace. Closing her eyes, she leaned back in her seat and relaxed.

She must have dozed off because when she opened her eyes, Lucas was carrying her into the elevator. Over his shoulder she caught the two doormen watching with avid interest. She ducked into his chest, mortified.

As the doors closed with them inside, she kicked her feet and patted his chest. "You can put me down now. I'm awake."

He looked down at her, his gaze tracing her features, settling on her mouth. "Not just yet."

"I'm fine. Really."

"Maybe I'm not."

"Lucas," she whispered, the feel of their bodies pressed together stealing her breath.

He lifted her closer, his intent clear, and then at the last moment he glanced away as the doors whooshed open. Once across the threshold, he lowered her gently to the ground and immediately took himself off to the kitchen, mumbling something about menus and coupons. The moment was over with the elevator ride, but its effect left her out of breath and trembling. She put a hand out, catching the edge of the entry table, needing the support.

She caught her reflection in the mirror. Placing her hands on her flushed cheeks, she mentally chided herself. *You're an idiot. You want him. He wants you. Go for it!*

She'd do it. Tonight. After dinner. No, at bedtime. She'd just follow him into his room very seductive-like. Except she didn't do seductive or anything resembling it.

"I've got two menus," Lucas said from behind her, causing her to jump and yelp in surprise, knocking a box off the table.

She bent to pick it up at the same time he reached for it. At the sight of his hand covering hers on the box, heat flooded her, and a burst of pure lust detonated the last of her reserve. She threw herself at him. He caught her deftly, tumbling them over until he lay on top of her. He stared down at her with eyes full of the pent up longing that threatened to consume her. This time he didn't give her a chance to reject him and set his mouth to hers with the determination of a man who would not be turned away.

His kiss was hot and fierce, lighting an answering fire within her. She clung to him, wrapping her arms and legs around him, pressing his pelvis into hers. He groaned. Or was that her? His hand stole up under her shirt and some of his control seemed to slip on a moan as he palmed her bare breast.

"You're not wearing a bra, *querida*," he murmured against her throat.

"No."

"Thank God."

He traced circles around the tip of her breast with his thumb, closer and closer, but not quite giving her what she wanted. She threw an arm up, arching her back. With a low growl he shoved her shirt up. He stopped everything and just stared at her bared breasts. She grew nervous, hoping he wasn't disappointed.

"They're so small," he whispered.

Mortification washing over her, she tried to push her shirt back down, but he held it tight.

"No. Don't. Let me." And then he bent his head and sucked nearly her whole breast into his mouth, his tongue playing with her hardened nipple.

She lurched up, stunned by the erotic pull. She clasped the back of his head, fastening him to her, and writhed against him. He unbuttoned her jeans and slid his large hand past her panties. His groan at finding her hot and wet for him reverberated through her breast. She gripped his wrist, wanting his fingers inside her. He slid across her slick folds as she guided him and caught her rhythm.

Adding his own trick, he used his thumb, hitting her at just the right spot. Once, twice...she bucked and came so hard she dug her fingers into his wrist, crying out. He cupped her mound, holding in, and extending the sensations that barreled through her, all the while whispering of her beauty and the things he wanted to do to her. She clung to him as the quivering subsided. He gathered her face in his hands and kissed her as though she'd given him a great gift.

She relaxed her hold and soothed the marks she'd no doubt made on him.

Panting a little as though he'd run the race with her, he looked down at her. "Bedroom. Now."

"Oh, *yes.*"

She scrambled out from under him, accidentally kicking the box with her foot. It skidded across the shiny tile floor, hit the wall, and bounced back to her. She picked it up to put it back on the table and froze.

In bold, block letters the address label read: To Mrs. Doyle Gann.

fter two agonizing hours they were allowed back into the apartment. The bomb squad had cleared the package. Whatever was inside was not explosive or made of explosive material. And now they stood in Lucas's living room, staring at the box sitting on his coffee table as if it *would* explode.

Detective Rolls flipped his notebook closed. "Do you want to open it before we take it in?"

"No," Lucas responded at the same time Mi said, "Yes."

"Well, which is it?"

Mi huddled as close to Lucas as she could, her arms wrapped around herself. He had thrown an arm across her shoulders, claiming her, and brought her tight up against his side. He was looking at her now to give her permission to open the box.

"Open it," she said as though they were talking about a coffin instead of a six-by-six inch cardboard box.

Rolls snapped on a pair of latex gloves and pulled out a pocketknife. The box had already been photographed from every angle and now the photographer stood ready to document its contents.

With the care and skill of a plastic surgeon, Rolls deftly sliced open the bottom. He lifted back the flaps, flattening them down with both hands. Then he placed his palm over the opening and up-ended the box, releasing the contents into his hand. He lifted the box away, a square of neatly folded tissue paper sitting in his palm. He set it on the table and peeled back the layers to reveal a circle of fine brown lace large enough to be worn around the neck.

As one, they leaned forward for a better look.

"Is that—" Rolls broke off.

Mi clamped a hand over her mouth, bile rising up the back of her throat.

"Jesus," Lucas breathed.

The artist had painstakingly woven the dark strands into an intricate floral design. It was delicate, dainty, and obviously meant to be worn proudly as the exquisite piece of art it was. Up close, thin threads of gold and bronze wove through the chocolate.

The son of a bitch had sent her a necklace made of hair. Her hair.

The flash from the photographer's camera played tricks with Mi's eyes, making her dizzy. Gagging, she pushed away from Lucas. She ran down the hall to the bathroom, barely making it in time to be sick. Wracked, her body heaved the meager contents of her stomach into the toilet.

Lucas stood outside the bathroom door, his forehead and palm pressed against it, listening to Mi's pitiful retching. Useless. That's what he was. The bastard had found a way to get to her despite his precautions. And now she was paying the price for his carelessness.

"Mi, open the door for me." He thumped his palm on the door. "*Querida*, please." He heard the toilet flush, then the water in the sink. After a few moments, the door handle rattled.

Her face was pale, her lips moist and red. He reached for her, drawing her into his embrace. She carried the minty tang of toothpaste, her skin and clothes damp with the sweat of exertion. She trembled as though cold, shaking with the effort to hold herself together.

"*Mi guerrera valiente*," he whispered more to himself than her. His valiant warrior.

"Wh... why would he s-s-send me that?"

"I don't know." Smoothing a hand down her hair, he kissed the top of her head. "Come lay down, *querida*." He picked her up and took her to his big bed. He laid her down amongst the mound of pillows and took off her shoes. She looked so small. "I'll get rid of the detective. You rest." He kissed her lightly and closed the door behind him.

Mi curled onto her side away from the door. A moment later the door opened again, the bed dipped, and then she was gazing into Gooch's big blue eyes.

"Here." He tucked the kitten against her and with a last kiss on her cheek he left.

As though knowing just what she needed, Gooch snuggled into her embrace, purring like a lion. She closed her eyes, focusing on the moment and the feel of the kitten's warm furry body.

Some time later, Lucas roused her from sleep. "I made some soup. We never did get that pizza you wanted."

She sighed and stretched, dislodging Gooch, who protested loudly and launched himself off the bed. She followed Lucas to the kitchen. He'd set out two bowls of tomato soup, plates of grilled cheese sandwiches, and glasses of milk.

"You cooked," she said, sliding onto a barstool.

"I opened a can and slapped some cheese between slices of bread. I wouldn't call that cooking."

"I would." She bit into a sandwich. The cheese was creamy and salty, oozing out the sides just the way she liked it. "Mmm, so good."

He gave her a shy kind of smile, as though her compliment had embarrassed him. They ate in companionable silence, more out of hunger than a lack of something to say. After polishing off her second sandwich, Mi asked the question that troubled her the most.

"Why me?"

Lucas examined the remains of his soup bowl for a moment before answering. "There's no way to know why. Only Doyle Gann knows. For whatever reason you attracted his attention." He put his hand over hers in her lap. "You did nothing to deserve this. You didn't cause this."

"I know that. I do. But I still don't get the why. Why *me*? I'm not special or pretty or rich or even especially famous. *So why me*?"

"I think you're pretty." He leaned in and kissed her. "I don't care if you're rich or especially famous." He kissed her again. "You're special to me."

She placed a hand to his cheek and looked into the dark eyes that had riveted her from the first moment their gazes had met. How could she have not thought him handsome? He was everything that was masculine and good, kind and sexy, strong and caring. And he wanted her.

God above, she wanted him.

Taking his hand, she slipped down from her barstool and drew him off his. Without a word, she towed him to the big bedroom at the end of the hall. When she'd imagined them together, she'd pictured them here in his big bed with the walls of windows. Stopping at the side of the bed, she turned to face him. She reached for the hem of her shirt and pulled it over her head. The city lights twinkling in the distance were the only illumination, but she could clearly make out his expression as his gaze roamed over her bare skin.

God damn, but she was beautiful, Lucas thought, shucking his shirt in one fluid motion. He couldn't take his eyes off of her. She glowed. The golden light gilded her skin, like the statue of a goddess, the gentle slope of her breasts the only shadow. She reached for the button of her jeans. His eyes followed the motion. Then she was standing before him in nothing but the smallest scrap of lace. He wasted no time following suit, kicking off his shoes and shedding his jeans. He didn't dare look away from her. If she were going to retreat from him, he'd have to find a way to convince her to stay.

He stood before her, bare in more ways than one, wanting nothing more than the feel of her skin on his. She moved toward him, her lips curved into a coy smile as though she knew she had all the power. And damned if she didn't. She put her hands on him, rising up on her toes to smooth her palms over his pecs, across his shoulders, down his arms and back again. He shuddered and she repeated the motion, adding a sweet little purring sound that locked the breath in his throat.

"Touch me," she begged in the softest voice.

He dropped to his knees before her, giving her the advantage of height. He reached for her, bringing her against him. The feel of her skin on his nearly broke him, her kiss inflaming him to the point of madness. She threaded her fingers through his hair. He couldn't stop touching her, kissing her, licking her, pressing her to him. He wanted to be everywhere at once.

Her breasts, a miniature perfection, drew his immediate attention. With a hand on her ass, he clasped her to him. He traced a finger over the slight slope, down and around, closer each time, watching in fascination as her nipple pebbled for him just inches away. He'd never seen breasts so small and hadn't thought size much mattered. But hers... Jesus. He flicked his tongue out for a taste. She moaned and arched. So sensitive. He licked again, holding her as she leaned back, offering more. He took it. Her nipple in his mouth...

He could smell her. God he wanted her. Bare. All of her. Gripping the scrap of lace covering her, he yanked. The material ripped, gave way. She whimpered, her knees buckling as he slipped a finger in from behind. She was so hot, so wet, the scent of her... aw, damn. Had to have her. Had to taste her. *Now*.

He lifted her and threw back the covers, placing her close to the edge of the bed. She spread wide for him and he got his first look at her. So beautiful. His. She made a small noise as he knelt before her. One lick and she jerked, gripping the bed sheets. And then he set his mouth to her, loving her. She writhed and moaned, pressing her feet against his shoulders. He slipped in one finger, then another. Working her with his tongue and mouth he took his time, stimulating and soothing, he brought her to the edge.

"Oh, God," she begged. "Oh, my God. Oh, oh, ah..."

He sucked gently, swirling his tongue, pistoning his fingers and she came hard for him with a long low moan. He nearly lost it, holding on to her through her last shudders.

Had to be in her. *Now*. He stripped the rest of the way and reached into the bedside drawer. The condom secured, he returned to her. He nibbled her inner thigh and she twitched, reaching for him. He stretched out next to her, watching as he smoothed a hand up her thigh, over the flat of her stomach and back again.

She pulled him down for a kiss and he knew she could smell herself on him. Running her hands over him, she shifted and then he was there. Right there. Between her legs. He looked down. He had to go slow for her. Had to make it good. He held himself over her, careful to not crush her. She moved beneath him, tilting her hips in invitation. He gripped himself and spread her moisture to lubricate his entrance. He hesitated, unsure. She was *so small.*

"Please tell me you've done this before."

He looked up at her. "What?"

She leaned up on her elbows, getting her first good look at him. "You're big, but you'll fit. You have done this before, right?"

Her words finally sank in. He didn't know whether to laugh or be annoyed. "Yes. Of course."

"Then get on with it!"

He blinked down at her. Then with care he positioned himself and pushed. She gave. He took a breath, his muscles straining with the effort to keep from crushing her and thrust a little deeper. Damn, she felt good. She moaned. Using her grip on his ass, she tilted and pushed him in a little more. He stilled, absorbing the incredible feeling of finally being inside her.

She pinched his ass. "Don't stop. Please move. Now." She added a smack. *"Hard."*

He exhaled in a whoosh, driving deep within her. He got lost in the frenzy, pumping fast and hard. She cried out for God, demanding he go harder, faster, harder. He changed his grip, her legs thrown over his arms. And hit deep. She screamed his name. He plunged into her grabbing the bed, her, anything, as he came hard into her.

He dropped, collapsing in a heap on top of her, but Mi didn't care. He'd finally lost control. She'd made the great Lucas Vega lose control. And oh, my God it had been amazing. She gasped for breath. She knew he'd be good, but oh!

Man he was heavy. She poked his arm. Nothing. She squeezed her inner muscles. *That* got his attention.

With a grunt he shifted his weight to one side. "Sorry."

She sighed.

"Are you all right, *querida*?" He caressed her cheek. "I didn't hurt you did I?"

"Yes. And I'm hoping you'll do it again in a few minutes."

He flinched, then her meaning seemed to sink in. "You're teasing." His grin started slow, spreading to his eyes. He palmed her breast, lazily flicking his thumb over her nipple. He licked the shell of her ear and she trembled. "On one condition."

She squirmed, shifting for better access to his body. "Anything."

"You're with me and only me, *querida*." He nipped her lobe, then sucked on the sting. "Say it."

God, he barely touched her and she wanted him all over again. His mouth moved down her throat, kissing, nibbling. She tried to turn into him, but he held her down with one strong leg over hers. By slow torture his mouth found her breast, his hand stroking down her stomach, then lower. He slipped a finger inside, then out in a slow, agonizing motion that made her whimper. And then his mouth was on her breast and he sucked hard, deep. She flexed her hips, wanting, needing more. She was right there...

"Say it, *querida*."

"*Yes*."

"Say it." He quickened the pace.

"Oh, *God*, yes."

He pulled her nipple in deep, flicked just the right spot and she came in a sharp, limb-numbing orgasm that rocked her into another universe.

He held her, gently soothing, coaxing. "*Querida*," he barely whispered the almost plea.

"Yes, Lucas," she near sobbed. "Only you."

He kissed her, a firm seal on her promise, and then he was gone. A moment later the bed dipped and he was there between her legs, gathering her to him.

"I want you again." She felt his tentative invasion. "I have to have you. Forgive me." With a growl, he plunged deep, gripping her hip. He set a wicked pace, kissing her with equal fervor, whispering endearments in two languages. She could hardly keep up. She came again, but he held off, driving into her with a relenting force that demanded everything from her. As though he were trying to imprint himself on her with every thrust, he made her *feel* him. Understanding dawned. He was claiming her, commanding her to be his.

She pushed on him and he rolled them. Now she was on top. His gaze was hot and fierce, glittering up at her, daring her. She gripped his shoulders as he'd gripped her hips and rose up, then down, matching his intensity. Sweat beaded her brow, but she wouldn't back down. She knew she couldn't just say the words, that wouldn't be enough. She had to declare them with her body. His. Only his. And in return, he was hers. Only hers.

He smoothed a hand up her thigh to where they were joined and used his thumb to touch her there, just there. Throwing her head back, she went off, crying out. He held her fast to him and pushed deep, grinding his release into her with a rumbling groan that vibrated through her.

They clung to each other, panting. She might have dozed, she wasn't sure. Loose limbed, she couldn't move if she tried. Or speak. She lay sprawled on top of him, arms and legs akimbo. He didn't seem to mind. She should probably move. Or say something.

As their heated bodies cooled, reality set in. She opened her eyes to the perfect view of the sparkling Dallas skyline. Soon it would be morning. Dawn would bring back her problems along with the scorching summer sun. In the meantime, she had the twinkling lights and the strong, steady heartbeat of the man beneath her.

He caressed her back, languidly smoothing a hand down then up. He sighed and shifted. She propped her chin on her hand and looked up at him. His eyes were closed, but there was the faintest of smiles curving his lips. He seemed very pleased with himself. As he should be. Hell, she was pretty pleased herself.

They'd knocked together like a couple of crazed teenagers. She was bound to be sore in some very inconvenient places. A good kind of sore. The best kind. She touched a fingertip to a mark on his chest.

She'd bitten him. Huh. She resisted the urge to turn him over and examine the scratch marks she was sure were there. He probably looked like he'd slept with Wolverine. She suppressed a giggle at the thought.

"What's so funny?" He raised his other arm and reached for a pillow, pulling it down under his head. His dark eyes open, watching her.

"I was just thinking that your back probably looks like you slept with Wolverine, you know, the scratch marks. I hope I didn't hurt you."

"Huh, not likely." He brushed a lock of hair behind her ear. "Are you hurt?"

"I'll be, uh, sore. In a good way," she quickly added. "But otherwise no. You're not the brute you think you are, you know."

"No?" He didn't seem convinced.

"You can have a look. Examine me from head to toe. I bet there's not a mark on me." She touched the bite on his chest. "I wasn't so gentle with you."

He chuckled. "I'll take you up on that exam later. When I can move."

"Can I ask you something?"

"Sure."

"Why did you and Vanessa break up?"

He tensed at the name. "It's complicated."

She was immediately sorry for asking the question and then just as suddenly she knew the answer, could feel it vibrating off of him. "She cheated."

"Yeah."

She waited with the feeling there was more to the

story and a rising dislike for the cool, red-haired beauty.

"With her personal trainer. She got pregnant."

"Obviously not yours."

"No." His expression made it clear the subject was closed.

She made a quick topic change, opting for neutral ground. "Who do you think is behind the sabotage at the station?"

"My turn to ask a question."

She tried to hide her reticence. "Shoot."

"Who called you yesterday?"

"Yesterday?" Her heart sped up, cold dread pricked from the inside out.

"Yesterday morning. You came in here to take the call and then when you came out you were upset."

She rolled her bottom lip between her teeth and thought hard about what to say. Finally she decided to go with the truth... mostly. "My mom."

"Your mom."

"Yes."

"And?"

"And, well, she hasn't been feeling well. I had asked Jason to keep an eye on her for me." Her useless brother hadn't ever gone by, only called. Once.

"Do you want to check on her tomorrow?"

"No."

"No?" Incredulity turned that small word into a condemnation.

"It's okay, really. Forget about it." She scooted off of him, off of the bed. "Hey, you know what? I am starved." She backed toward the bathroom. "Didn't you say there was a Chinese place that delivers late?" She closed the bathroom door, ending the discussion she'd so stupidly started.

Lucas leaned up on his elbows and watched her go with that same sinking feeling he had when Malcolm had told him what he'd found out about her. He flopped back on the bed. The lights from the city dotted ceiling, creating an artificial constellation overhead.

What was she hiding? He scrubbed his hands over his face. Whatever it was, she wasn't going to tell him willingly, maybe never. He rolled up into a sitting position, hanging his hands between his knees over the edge of the bed. He stared at the door, willing it to open and for her to come out and confess all to him.

Again he was tempted to call Malcolm and ask him to dig deeper into Mi's background. He hated not knowing. Hated not being able to trust her. Hated that this situation reminded him of what he'd gone through with Vanessa.

Fuck it all. Why couldn't he pick women who were an open book? With nothing to hide, no reason to lie?

He got up and took care of the spent condom. Washing his hands in the spare bathroom, he glanced at his reflection in the mirror. She was right. He turned to examine the long line of scratches down his back. She'd left her mark on him in more ways than one. He leaned forward, one, two, three bite marks on his chest. Huh. He hadn't felt them. Damn, she was a wild little thing. Frenzied and uninhibited, she'd knocked his world sideways. But it was the sharp contrast of her blunt honesty in bed and her secretiveness out of it that really threw him. What was he going to do with her?

Thinking about her got him hard all over again. But he'd have to wait and in the meantime figure out some way to gain her trust.

9

L ucas wasn't sure which was more frustrating: the lack of leads on Doyle Gann's where-abouts or Mi's habit of moving his things around his closet just to see if he'd notice. He noticed. Then he'd move them back only to find she'd moved something else the next time he went in there.

He couldn't figure out what she'd done this time, but something was definitely off. He counted his shirts. All there. Pants. Check. Then he turned to the shoes. Damn it. One pair was missing. He rummaged around and finally found them at the bottom of the clothes hamper. Grinning like an idiot, he put them back on the shelf where they belonged. He actually *liked* this game of hers. What was wrong with him?

Now that he'd figured out her trick of the day, he grabbed the pair of shoes he intended to wear and walked out into the living area. She wasn't there, but the siren call of pancakes led him right to her, standing at the stove holding a spatula in nothing but an old t-shirt of his. It was so old and thin he could see through it, which was how he knew she had nothing else on. God bless cheap cotton.

"Aren't you going to be late for work?" he asked, making a show of checking his watch.

It was Monday morning and they'd spent nearly all weekend in bed. But still, just the sight of her in that ragged t-shirt, her nipples clearly defined by the thin fabric, had him wondering what she'd do if he lifted her onto the counter top and stepped between her legs.

"Crosby called while you were in the shower. The shipment that was supposed to come in on Friday, came in today and it was all wrong. They sent Davy to the warehouse in Fort Worth to pick up the missing products for tonight's show. So we have another hour or so before we have to leave." She flipped a pancake. "Hungry?"

"Yes."

"Good. Why don't you get the plates and set them up at the bar?"

"Sure." He turned and left the room.

"Ah, Lucas," he heard her call after him. "The plates are in here!"

He returned a moment later and reached past her to turn the stove off.

"What are you doing? I wasn't done cooking."

In answer he wrapped his arms around her from behind, pressing his erection against her.

"Are you serious? I have to leave for work in less than an hour and I haven't even showered yet." He nibbled her neck, his hands roaming north and south.

She made that little sighing squeak sound he loved. "All right, but make it quick. And good. It better be good."

He found her already wet for him and moaned at the feel of her heat. He moved her away from the stove and lifted her onto the counter, wedging between her legs as he'd imagined. He slapped a condom down on the counter next to her and kissed her long and deep until she was squirming against him.

"You're a naughty boy," she panted, giving him a playful whack on the backside with the spatula.

He grabbed a fistful of her shirt in back and pulled it tight across her chest. Dipping his head, he captured her nipple in his mouth, sucking through the thin cotton. She gasped, and reached for the fastening of his pants as the spatula clattered to the floor. She managed to get both hands on him, stroking him. She spread a bead of moisture across the tip with her thumb. He patted the counter blindly, searching for the condom, his mouth now at her other breast.

"Looking for this?"

He broke away to find her twirling the condom between two fingers. He reached for it.

"Nuh-uh. I'll do it." She bit the edge of the foil and tore slowly, a naughty glint in her eye.

Damn, she was hot.

Using her feet she pushed his pants down where they pooled at his ankles. She scooted to the edge of the counter. "Now hold real still. I want to make sure I get this on just right."

He widened his stance, gripping her thighs for balance. She made a show of getting the condom on right side up, faking a couple of false starts. He shifted his feet, watching her every move. She turned it one way, then the other swirling it over the crown, teasing him. She used both hands to roll it all the way down, slow as if she had all the time in the world. Wrapping both hands around him, she smoothed up then down, up, then down...

"It's on," he bit out.

"Just making sure." She blinked up at him all wide innocent eyes.

Two could play at that game.

"I'm ready. Are you?" He asked, sliding a hand up her thigh. Gliding a finger across her slickness, he pretended not to notice how incredibly *ready* she was. Her breath caught, her fingers flexing on his shoulders. "No. Hmm. Maybe if I did this." He used two fingers on her, scissoring over and around, but not quite doing what she needed.

"Oh, God, yes. That. Do that. Faster."

"Faster?" He sped up just a little.

Wrapping her legs around his, she panted and arched her back. Reaching out, she grabbed a cabinet knob with each hand. "In me now."

"I don't think you're ready," he rasped, nearing the end of his control. He shoved her shirt up, pinning it to the cabinet over her shoulder. He licked the exposed nipple.

Her breathing grew rough, but still he held her right on the edge. He varied the rhythm, playing with her, never letting her get too close to coming. He wet her nipple with his mouth, but didn't suck.

"God, damn it, Lucas. Do it now. *Please*."

That did it. He withdrew his fingers from her, grabbed his dick, and thrust hard. She gasped at the intrusion. He pumped into her, holding her still with both hands. She chanted his name, but he knew she wasn't quite there... he bent his head, sucked her breast, flicked the nipple, and she cried out. His orgasm slammed into him, weakening his knees. He held onto the counter, afraid he'd crumple to the floor and take her with him.

Her head flopped forward against his chest. He curled around her and they held each other as if they were the only survivors of a shipwreck.

"Okay, that was *good*."

He let out an exhausted laugh. "Glad to be of service."

"But if you don't let me up I'm going to have to tell Crosby why I'm late."

He looked down to where they were joined, then pulled out slowly. He always hated leaving her.

She watched too. "I still have no idea how you fit. I thought for sure you were going split me in two that first time."

"I hurt you?"

"A little," she confessed.

"*What*?" His head jerked back as if he'd been punched. "Jesus, why didn't you tell me?"

"It had been a long time for me and I didn't know it would hurt that much." She shrugged it off. "I lived and we went on to have some pretty spectacular sex. It was worth it. Don't you think?"

"No." He bent over and pulled up his pants. He remembered that second time when he'd practically taken her without her permission. He'd been rough, thinking only of his needs. His stomach knotted, he thought he might be sick.

He didn't know where to look, what to do. "Do you still... does it still..."

She clasped a hand around his wrist, shackling him in place. "No."

He looked down at their hands his so much bigger than hers and swallowed back the bile. He knew what damage big hands could do. "That second time—"

"I was sore at first and then, well, it was really good." She smiled. "I forgot all about the pain."

He moaned and turned his head away as though her pain was his. He couldn't stand the thought of her hurting... because of him. Vanessa's last words came back to him. *You're a shark, cold and flat, taking bites out of people until there's nothing left.*

Pulling out of her grip, he backed away, unable to meet her eyes. He didn't want to be like that. He'd worked so *hard* not to be that.

"Lucas—" She reached for him.

He put a hand up. "Please, don't." Self-loathing, his old friend, burned a hole in his gut. He could hardly get the words out. "If I ever... you have to promise me..."

"Anything."

He would have to work harder, he told himself. And if he failed... he couldn't fail. He *wouldn't* fail. His voice strengthened with his resolve. "You have to tell me."

Mi struggled to understand. "Okay."

He went to her then, looking down at her with eyes full of earnest anguish that pierced her chest. Had she done this to him?

"You tell me if I hurt you," he said. "I need to know. Promise me you'll tell me."

"I will."

"Don't wait. Not ever again."

"I won't. I promise."

He nodded and stepped away. She watched him go, wanting to kick herself for her stupidity. What had she done?

Lucas kept his distance from her as though he didn't trust himself. The whole time Mi was getting ready to go to the studio, she went over in her head everything that had happened between them, especially what had happened in the kitchen. She didn't understand why he was upset. She had known he was worried about how much bigger and taller he was than her, but she thought he'd gotten over it. She didn't understand what the big deal was. His reaction... the look in his eyes... agonized.

She sneaked a peek at his profile. He was focused on the road, a wrist resting across the top of the steering wheel, his other hand absently rubbing his thigh. He tended to do that when he was thinking. She'd seen the scars there and although he'd brushed them off as no big deal, she had a feeling they went much deeper than the shiny, gnarled skin.

They turned onto the street for the studio. The sound hit them, like a blast in the face, chants of morality and family values. Picket signs swayed in time to the beat, the faces distorted into masks of hatred and intolerance. The crowd had doubled yet again in size and lined both sides of the street. Barricades had been placed to keep people off the street. The few protestors who broke through them were quickly shoved back by Cal's security guards.

Lucas tensed, transforming into what Mi called his defender mode. He sat up straighter, his gaze constantly scanning the mirrors of the truck and the area around them. Tightening his grip on the wheel, he pulled his gun and laid it across his lap. "Get down," he ordered.

She was already folding herself into the small space under the dashboard before the words had left his mouth. Squeezing into a tight ball, she closed her eyes, her hands automatically covering her ears. "I pledge allegiance to the flag..." She didn't know how many times she recited it until she finally felt Lucas's hand on her arm.

"Come on out of there," he said, concern raking lines in his forehead.

He didn't joke it off as he'd done the last time. Instead he drew her into his arms, hiding his face in the side of her neck as though he was the one who needed comforting. She hugged him hard. His heart beat wild and erratic against hers.

A knocking on Mi's window broke them apart. They turned to find Cal smirking at them. His honey stood just behind him, tapping on a laptop tablet she held like a clipboard. Lucas got out of the truck and came around to Mi's side. He opened the door and helped her down.

Cal kept quiet, assessing their every move with cool blue eyes that missed nothing. "Good morning," he finally said. "Have a pleasant weekend?"

"Your crowd control is barely holding," Lucas replied over his shoulder as he escorted Mi into the building with a hand on her back.

Cal followed, as did his honey, the click-clack of her high heels echoing off the walls of the hall.

"I know," Cal said, his tone flat and rigid. "We need to talk."

Mi ducked into the make-up room so Lucas and Cal could speak privately. Tracey was already there, looking annoyed. "Where have you been?" She gave Mi a look that said she knew exactly where Mi had been and what—or rather—who she'd been doing.

Mi bit the inside of her cheek, trying not to snipe back. Her tolerance for Tracey's attitude toward Lucas was wearing thin. "What exactly is it about Lucas you don't like?"

Tracey wandered over to the makeup counter and busied herself rearranging the items on top. "I don't know what you're talking about."

Mi put a hand on Tracey's, stilling her movements. "Yes. You do." She gave Tracey's hand a gentle squeeze, drawing her friend's attention. "Why don't you like him?"

"I never said I didn't like him."

"Then what's the deal?"

"He's... scary."

"Lucas? Are you serious?"

Tracey nodded. "He scares the crap out of me. I don't like that he comes here every day with you. And since I'm being honest, I don't really believe he's your boyfriend."

Mi wasn't too sure what she and Lucas were, what label to put on it, but boyfriend and girlfriend fit as good as any for now. Whether or not they would stay together after this forced involvement she wasn't sure. When they were alone she could pretend they had a future, at least until her brother showed up or her mother called.

"He's in my life. He's important to me. Please try to understand and respect that," Mi said with a quiet bid for her friend's approval.

"So you really are together?"

"Yes. We are." *For now*.

"Oh. Well, okay then. I'm sorry."

"Thank you." Mi pressed Tracey's hand one last time, then sat down to get ready for the show.

Tracey started work on her hair. They made small talk about the show, Tracey's new apartment, and other things, but the specter of Tracey's disapproval hung over their conversation. Mi wondered if her friend would get over her trepidation once she got to know Lucas or if it even mattered since he might not be around once the threats against her were resolved.

Mi put thoughts of the future and Lucas aside to focus on preparing for the show. There had been some changes to the lineup of products she'd be featuring for the show that would air tonight. Something about marketing and the all of the publicity the protesters were garnering for the show. They'd added a few more high end products to boost the show's sales numbers. Usually they promoted these products around holidays. There were a few new ones Mi wasn't familiar with, so she took a few moments to fiddle with them, learning how the switches worked. She jotted notes about a couple of them on her cards.

Just before they were set to begin taping, Davy rushed over and switched out a standard vibrator that usually sold well for one Mi had never seen before. "I guess this one just came out. It's called iLuv. It's Internet enabled. Here's the card." He handed her the new vibrator's information card.

"Thanks, Davy."

"Sure." He started to step off the stage, then turned back with a shy smile. "Hey, I just wanted to tell you how pretty you look today, Miss Mi."

She blinked up at him, surprised.

"I don't mean nothing by it. I know you're with that big guy and all. I just wanted to tell you that you look real nice. Happy. It's good to see you happy."

"Thank you, Davy."

"Okay, well... have a good show." He put up a hand in wave.

She stared after him a moment, then with a small smile and shake of her head returned to the cards in her hands.

"Two minutes!" Crosby barked.

Mi examined the new vibrator, reading the features off the card. She tried to get it to work, but it wouldn't. She looked around for Davy. She found him sitting at a table, hunched over a laptop in a far corner of the studio.

"Hey, Davy! This isn't working," she told him.

"I know." He gave her a bashful grin. "I'm going to work it from this laptop." He hit a command and the vibrator's clitoral stimulator buzzed to life.

"Oh, my gosh!" Mi gushed. "That is so cool. Make it do something else."

He tapped a couple more keys and the shaft thrust up and down.

"We have got to synchronize this to the sales pitch," she said. He came over and they worked out a few prompt words that would match with computer commands from Davy.

"Let's go people. Places!" Crosby announced.

Tracey ran up onto the stage to give Mi one last pat with the powder puff. Then the countdown started and taping began.

Mi gave her usual introductory speech and then launched into the products she'd be showcasing today.

"We'll start our show this evening with an amazing bundle at an incredible price." She held up three items for the camera, transferring them from one hand to the other as she read off their names. "You'll get all three products: Indulgence's Stand Up and Salute multi-speed vibrator, the Double Your Pleasure bullets, and an eight ounce bottle of Love Water lubricant. All three of these products together are normally one thirty-three ninety-five, but tonight you can get all three for only ninety-nine ninety-five, a substantial savings."

She brought a red, white and blue striped vibrator into camera view.

"Indulgence's Stand Up and Salute, multi-speed vibrator is molded directly from adult film star Slade Rockum's erect member and made from a supple, flesh-like jelly that warms to the body. This rigid yet flexible vibe will bend to your will and is completely water-proof, making it perfect for when you want to play in the bath or shower."

She showed a plastic case with two silver bullets about the size of a AA battery attached to a wired controller.

"Also in tonight's bundle is Indulgence's Double Your Pleasure, two bullets for dual play on one controller. These bullets are discreet enough to take anywhere yet powerful enough to deliver incredible vibrating sensations. Use alone or with a partner for double your pleasure, double your fun, double pene-tration."

She held up a clear bottle with pink and red hearts on it.

"To ease play we've rounded out tonight's bundle with Indulgence's Love Water, a non-sticky, non-stain-ing, multi-use, water based lubricant." She showed all three at once. "You get all three of these wonderful products for only ninety-nine ninety-five, tonight only."

She set aside the product bundle and picked up a purple vibrator embedded with glitter that made it sparkle under the studio lights.

"We have a real treat for you tonight, for the first time on *Pleasure at Home* we have a wonderful new product: the iLuv Internet enabled vibrator. Control your partner's pleasure remotely from anywhere around the world. Thrust—" The shaft moved up and down thanks to Davy. "Stimulate—" The double tipped clitoral stimulator vibrated just as they'd planned before the show. "Pulse—" The beads in the shaft rotated clockwise then counterclockwise.

"This extraordinary vibrator takes gratification into the next millennium and

be—"

BANG. The heat hit first. A blinding, scotching wind that knocked everything backwards. She hit hard. Body, then head smacked. A sharp pain gripped her side. No noise. Hot debris rained down. She tried to sit up, but something held her legs down. Smoke choked. Where was the noise? The sky opened up. Water fell in fat drops. But she was inside. A hand on her face.

She blinked through the smoke and water. Lucas's black smudged face swam into focus. Blood ran from his forehead over one eye. His lips moved, then he went away. Her legs were freed. He came back, running hands over her. Talking, but no sound. She tried to speak. Her voice came out as a croak. Her head ached. She closed her eyes and was lifted. Dizzy. So dizzy. Her stomach roiled. She took deep, smoke-stinging breaths and coughed. Choked.

She drifted into the wave of blackness that came for her.

Hands patted her face. She batted them away, but

they shook her. Lucas. She hurt. She tried to tell him. Her mouth moved. He shook his head, pointing to his ears. She tried to nod. The pain hit again. She moaned and turned away. He caught her face, bringing it back to him. But not before she saw. The fire. People. Some walking. Some hurt like her, some still. She twisted against his hands, wanting to know. He fought her, then released her with a frown. He said something.

She turned back to the building. Lucas motioned someone over. A paramedic bent down next to her. She pushed at him and pointed to a motionless form with long blond hair soaked and matted red. The paramedic shook his head, said something. A fireman approached the lifeless blond figure and draped a yellow tarp over it.

A sob clogged her throat. She reached a hand out, tried to move.

No. *No.*

Not Davy.

Please, not him.

*****

THANK YOU FOR READING LOST! The next book in the DANGEROUS LINES series is SAVED . Lucas and Mi's situation is dire, can they learn to trust each other and find their happily ever after?

➤CLICK HERE TO READ SAVED➤

If you enjoyed LOST, please consider leaving a

review on your favorite book site. Reviews help readers find books!

➤LOST (DANGEROUS LINES novel)➤

➤GOODREADS➤

Join my VIP Facebook group Babes with Books for exclusive sneak peeks at my upcoming books & other, members only, perks:

➤www.facebook.com/groups/BabesWithBooks-ReaderGroup

Sign up to receive my newsletter for new release alerts, exclusive bonus content, and giveaways!

➤**www.bethyarnall.com/newsletter**

Turn the page to read an excerpt from SAVED now!

EXCERPT FROM SAVED

Lucas watched Mi sleep. She looked so fragile and pale against the stark, white hospital sheets. He'd fanned her hair over the pillow, smoothing it away from her face. A bruise was just beginning to bloom on her cheek. He ran a fingertip lightly over it. Her bottom lip was cut. He touched his finger to it as well, willing it to heal, hoping she didn't hurt. He looked down to where her hand rested in his, so small.

He'd been through some shit—some real bad shit —and finding Mi through the chaos and smoke in the studio had been right up there. His chest tightened with the memory of the blast, of not being able to find her. And then when he finally did, she'd been half covered in debris from the set. He'd had a bad moment as he'd dropped down beside her. It was like Gooch all over again. And then she'd opened her eyes and his heart had taken a hard knock against his ribs.

Since then he wouldn't leave her and had made

them sew up the gash on his forehead at her bedside. She would be all right. He thanked God or whoever for that miracle. One of the light bars had fallen across her legs. Luckily the couch had taken the brunt of the hit, saving her from any broken bones. She'd hit her head, but escaped with only a slight concussion. There were other injuries, all minor. She'd be bruised and sore, but otherwise okay.

She was damn lucky. They both were. Others hadn't been so fortunate. A cameraman had been burned badly. Another's leg had been crushed. He was still in surgery. Crosby had a broken arm and a severe concussion. Cal had escaped with nothing more than cuts and bruises. His honey hadn't faired so well with cracked ribs and a broken collarbone. Almost no one had escaped unscathed. Considering the size and timing of the blast it was a miracle there wasn't more than the one fatality.

He kissed the back of Mi's hand, marveling at the gift of that simple gesture. Her eyelashes fluttered open. Her gaze searched, then settled on him. His heart felt ten times too big for his chest.

He squeezed her hand to hide the shaking. "Hey."

"Hey." She croaked. "Water?"

He scrambled for the cup the nurse had left. Pressing the straw to her lips, he sent out another silent message of gratitude. She took a few sips, then settled back on the pillow.

"You don't have any broken bones." He tried for cheerful. "Only a slight concussion. They want to keep you overnight for observation."

"I know. I was there when they poked and prodded."

"Right."

"Are you okay?"

"Me?"

Her expression softened at his astonishment. "Yes, you." She eyed the bandage on his forehead. "Is that all?"

He put a self-conscious hand over it. "Yeah. Pretty much."

A frown formed between her brows and she looked as though she was trying to riddle something out. "I'm not sure of what is real. I remember being thrown back, hitting. The heat. Then you were there. Did you take me outside?" He nodded to confirm her memory. She put her free hand up to her ear. "My ears are ringing."

"Mine too. It'll get better."

"Okay." She tried to bite her lip and winced, blinking at the pain. She took a breath. "I think I faded out some. I heard one of the nurses say something about a bomb?"

"Yeah. They think one of the ah, vibrator things had been rigged."

"But why? Why would someone do that to us?"

"People do some fucked up things." He placed her hand between both of his more for his comfort than hers. "For some very fucked up reasons."

"You're quite the philosopher."

"I'm glad you can joke." He grinned at her, feeling for the first time since the explosion that things might turn out all right. "I predict a full recovery."

She gave him a small smile, but the frown still lingered between her brows. "I need you to tell me. I need to know. I saw..." Her eyes filled with tears. "Davy." Her voice broke on a sob. "Is he... did he..." She clamped a hand over her mouth as though keeping the words in kept them from being true.

He rubbed her hand between his, wanting more than anything to not say the words he knew would grieve her. "He didn't make it."

Tears spilled, flowing down her cheeks and around her fingers. Behind her hand she asked, "Who... who else?"

"Just him."

She closed her eyes, her hand forming a fist that she bit. "Crosby?" she managed to squeak out.

"A concussion and broken arm. He'll be okay."

"Tracey?"

"I haven't seen her. She might have been taken to another hospital."

She averted her face, pulled her hand from his and turned away, curling into a ball. "Oh, God, Davy." Her slight frame shook with silent sobs.

He rose from his chair and stood over her, not knowing what to do. Uselessness and despair ate at him until he thought it would consume him. A fine sheen of cold sweat broke out across his forehead. He put a tentative hand out, then pulled it back. He racked his brain for the right words, but none came. Acting on instinct and desperation, he climbed into bed with her. She turned into him. Wrapping his body around her, he brought her in tight.

"I'm sorry, *querida*," he whispered. "I'm so, so sorry."

He'd failed her. He was supposed to protect her. Instead he'd left her exposed, wrongly thinking she'd be safe inside the studio. The cops hadn't said it, but the implication was that the bomb had been meant for Mi. Something about a phone call claiming responsibility and the fact that the product the bomb was in had moments before been on the table in front of Mi. Davy had saved her by switching it at the last moment. He'd lost his life in place of Mi's.

The thought of losing her sunk a hole so deep in him he could hardly breathe. The feel of her safe in his arms, trembling with shock and grief, was a gift he didn't deserve. She gripped the front of his torn and stained shirt, tugging handfuls of his chest hair. He focused on that small pain as a way back to now, back to what he needed to do.

*

Mi thought she'd dissolve under the weight of her despair. *Davy.* She fisted her hands in Lucas's shirt, trying to find her balance. Davy's face with his shy smile and gentle hazel eyes superimposed over the last image she had of him, lying limp and lifeless just feet away from her. Squeezing her eyes tight, she tried to blot out the memory. She sniffed and swiped at the tears, forcing them back. She never cried, hadn't cried once in the past thirteen years.

Smoothing the wrinkles in Lucas's shirt, she fought for her bearings, fought to make some kind of sense of what had happened. She let out a breath, so thankful for this big man who had come to mean more to her than he should. After the explosion, she'd tried to get to him. He was the first thing she'd thought of. And then suddenly he'd been there, filling her vision. She closed her eyes at the memory that burned so sweet amongst the horror.

She'd turned so easily into him, into the comfort he offered. She sought him out from the moment she opened her eyes in the morning until she closed them at night. She'd come to depend on him. And that scared her down to the deepest, quietest place inside her. She wanted him, could feel herself leaning hard on needing him. He deserved better than she had to offer. Which wasn't much more than her body and the beginnings of feelings she couldn't follow through on.

"I'm sorry about your friend."

He placed a hand on her cheek and swiped a tear with his thumb. She couldn't seem to keep the tears from flowing. He followed it with a kiss to her forehead.

"I just can't believe... he was so young." Her breath shuddered on a suppressed sob. "He would've turned twenty-one next week. Oh, God. His parents. Has anyone called them?"

"I'm sure the cops will take care of that."

She nodded.

He pulled away. "You should rest, *querida*." He climbed out of bed and moved to the window. Hooking a finger in the curtain, he looked out. "The media is camped out in front of the hospital. The explosion will make the news."

"I'm sure Cookie Dixon and the other members of C.A.L.M. will be thrilled." She swiped at another stray tear. "They'll probably get that law reinstated, banning the sale of adult toys in Texas. We'll all be out of jobs." Memories of flames and smoke coming out of the studio filled her mind. Another tear slipped down her cheek. "If we're not already."

"They're claiming responsibility for the explosion."

"God," she said on an exhale.

"The bomb had to have been put in place by someone on the inside."

She whipped her head to look at him, shocked. The pain nearly split her skull. She breathed past the pain. This was all so unbelievable. "One of us did this? Killed Davy?"

He nodded, still looking out the window.

"Who?"

"I wish I knew."

"Do the police?"

"I don't know. What little information I have I got from the detective who came to interview me earlier while you slept."

She lay back in the bed, overwhelmed by this new information. Someone she worked with, someone she saw everyday had tried to kill them. They'd been like a family. Which one of the faces she had thought of as a friend's had harbored a hatred so black they'd kill?

Detective Rolls pushed into the room. He looked like he'd pulled his outfit from the bottom of the hamper and then slept in it. Grimness floated in a cloud around him. The door whooshed closed behind him, bringing the stale scent of dinner trays from the hall into the room. He fixed his bunched up eyes on Mi and sighed. "You look pretty good, considerin'." He motioned toward the chair by the bed. "May I?"

She smoothed away the traces of tears and inclined her head. "Do you know who did this?"

"I wish. ATF recognized the bomb signature, but the guy's been dead more 'an ten years," Rolls said.

Lucas turned away from the window. "Apprentice?"

Rolls jerked in surprise, clamping a hand to his chest. "Jesus H. Christmas. How in the hell d'you do that? I didn't see ya at all. That some special forces shit?"

Lucas scowled in response.

"Apprentice?" Mi asked.

"Most bombers work alone, but if he was with a militant group, he might have had an apprentice, someone to pass his trade on to," Lucas answered.

"That's an angle ATF's trackin'." Rolls took out a notebook and pen. "I haveta ask ya some questions 'bout the bombing."

Mi leaned back against the pillows and pulled the sheet up higher on her chest.

"Are you cold?" Lucas asked her, starting toward the bed.

"No. I'm fine. Thank you. Go ahead with your questions, detective."

Rolls shifted in his seat as though he was settling in for good long while. "Start me off by tellin' me whatya did when ya got to the TV studio."

"From the time we walked in the door?"

"Uh-huh."

Mi smothered a sigh and told the detective everything she could remember. Lucas stayed by the window, alternately looking out and keeping an eye on her. He frowned when Mi described the blast.

"Can ya think of anyone who'd do this or help someone do this?" Rolls asked.

"No." She rubbed her forehead, straining to come up with a clue or something that might help. "I can't believe someone I worked with would do such a thing."

"That's enough," Lucas said, coming away from the window. "She needs to rest. We'll call if we think of anything else."

"Just one more thing," Mi said. "Can you tell me which hospital they took Tracey Casey to? She's the makeup artist for the show. And my friend."

Rolls consulted his notebook. "Casey, you say?"

Mi nodded.

"Don't see the name here. She at the studio when the bomb went off?"

Mi twisted the bed sheet. "Yes."

"She ain't listed as injured." He flipped through the pages some more. "That's odd. She ain't listed as a witness either. You're sure about her bein' there?"

Lucas stepped over. "She was there."

*

Want to read more?
➤One-click SAVED Now➤

If you loved LOST, you'll love the sexy, funny, award

nominated INNOCENT serial. Cora's brother was convicted of a murder he didn't commit and it's up to her to set him free. Inspired by real cases taken on by The Innocence Project.

★ Nominated in 2017 for the Romance Writers of America Rita® award★

➤One-click EPISODE ONE Now➤

Looking for something lighter and funny? Check out THE MISADVENTURES OF MAGGIE MAE series, starting with WAKE UP, MAGGIE, available now! Maggie has to keep her very inappropriate thoughts to herself about the FBI Special Agent assigned to protect her from a murderer.

➤One-click WAKE UP, MAGGIE Now➤

ALSO BY BETH YARNALL

Dangerous Lines

Lost

Saved

Fake

Real

Urge

Rare

Betray

Recovered Innocence

Liberate

Exonerate

Vindicate

Innocent Serial

Episode One

Episode Two

Episode Three

The Misadventures of Maggie Mae

Wake Up, Maggie

You're Mine, Maggie

Find Me, Maggie

Azalea March Mysteries

Dyed and Gone

Beth Writing as Betty Paper

Exposed

Captive

Tinsel

Piano Lessons

BETH'S BOOKS FOR WRITERS

Crafting Unputdownable Fiction series

Going Deep Into Deep Point of View

Making Description Work Hard For You

Some Like It Hot: Writing Sex and Romance

ABOUT THE AUTHOR

USA Today best selling author and Rita® finalist, Beth
Yarnall, writes mysteries, romantic suspense, and the
occasional hilarious tweet. She lives in Southern Cali-
fornia with her husband, two sons, and their rescue
dogs where she is hard at work on her next novel. For
more information about Beth and her novels please
visit her website- www.bethyarnall.com

facebook.com/bethyarnallauthor

amazon.com/author/bethyarnall

bookbub.com/authors/beth-yarnall